KT-549-713

EX LIBRIS

_____
NAME

BOOK THE FOURTH

THE MISERABLE MILL

A Series of Unfortunate Events

BOOK THE FOURTH

THE MISERABLE MILL

by

Lemony Snicket

Illustrated by
BRETT HELQUIST

TED SMART

First published in the USA 2000
by HarperCollins Children's Books
First published in Great Britain 2002
by Egmont Books Ltd
239 Kensington High Street, London W8 6SA
This edition published in Great Britain 2005
for The Book People Ltd
Hall Wood Avenue, Haydock, St Helens WA11 9UL

Published by arrangement with
HarperCollins Children's Books,
a division of HarperCollins Publishers, Inc.,
1350 Avenue of the Americas, New York,
New York 10019, USA

Text copyright © 2000 Lemony Snicket
Inside illustration copyright © 2000 Brett Helquist
Cover illustration copyright © 2002 Brett Helquist

The moral right of the cover illustrator
has been asserted

A CIP catalogue record for this title is available from
the British Library

Printed and bound in Italy

All rights reserved. No part of this publication may
be reproduced, stored in a retrieval system, or
transmitted, in any form or by any means, electronic,
mechanical, photocopying, recording or otherwise,
without the prior permission of the publisher and
copyright owner.

To Beatrice –

My love flew like a butterfly

Until death swooped down like a bat

As the poet Emma Montana McElroy said:

"That's the end of that."

One

Sometime during your life—in fact, very soon—
you may find yourself reading a book, and you
may notice that a book's first sentence can often
tell you what sort of story your book contains.
For instance, a book that began with the sentence "Once upon a time there was a family of
cunning little chipmunks who lived in a hollow
tree" would probably contain a story full of talking animals who get into all sorts of mischief. A
book that began with the sentence "Emily sat
down and looked at the stack of blueberry pan-
cakes her mother had prepared for her, but she
was too nervous about Camp Timbertops to eat
a bite" would probably contain a story full of

giggly girls who have a grand old time. And a book that began with the sentence "Gary smelled the leather of his brand-new catcher's mitt and waited impatiently for his best friend Larry to come around the corner" would probably contain a story full of sweaty boys who win some sort of trophy. And if you liked mischief, a grand old time, or trophies, you would know which book to read, and you could throw the rest of them away.

But this book begins with the sentence "The Baudelaire orphans looked out the grimy window of the train and gazed at the gloomy blackness of the Finite Forest, wondering if their lives would ever get any better," and you should be able to tell that the story that follows will be very different from the story of Gary or Emily or the family of cunning little chipmunks. And this is for the simple reason that the lives of Violet, Klaus, and Sunny Baudelaire are very different from most people's lives, with the main difference being the amount of unhappiness, horror, and despair. The three children have no time to get into all sorts of mischief, because misery follows them wherever they go. They have not had a grand old time since their parents died in a terrible fire. And the only trophy they would win would be some sort of First Prize for Wretchedness. It is atrociously unfair, of course, that the Baudelaires have so many troubles, but that is the way the story goes. So now that I've told you that the first sentence will be "The Baudelaire orphans looked out the grimy window of the train and gazed at the gloomy blackness of the Finite Forest, wondering if their lives would ever get any better," if you wish to avoid an unpleasant story you had best put this book down.

The Baudelaire orphans looked out the grimy window of the train and gazed at the gloomy blackness of the Finite Forest, wondering if their lives would ever get any better. An announcement over a crackly loudspeaker had just told them that in a few minutes they would arrive in the town of Paltryville, where their new caretaker lived, and they couldn't help wondering who in the world would want to live in such dark and eerie countryside. Violet, who was fourteen and the eldest Baudelaire, looked out at the trees of the forest, which were very tall and had practically no branches, so they looked almost like metal pipes instead of trees. Violet was an inventor, and was always designing machines and devices in her head, with her hair tied up in a ribbon to help her think, and as she gazed out at the trees she began work on a mechanism that would allow you to climb to the top of any tree, even if it were completely bare. Klaus, who was twelve, looked down at the forest floor, which was covered in brown, patchy moss. Klaus liked to read more than anything else, and he tried to remember what he had read about Paltryville mosses and whether any of them were edible. And Sunny, who was just an infant, looked out at the smoky gray sky that hung over the forest like a damp sweater. Sunny had four sharp teeth, and biting things with them was what interested her most, and she was eager to see what there was available to bite in the area. But even as Violet began planning her invention, and Klaus thought of his moss research, and Sunny opened and closed her mouth as a prebiting exercise, the Finite Forest looked so uninspiring that they couldn't help wondering if their new home would really be a pleasant one.

"What a lovely forest!" Mr. Poe remarked, and coughed into a white handkerchief. Mr. Poe was a banker who had been in charge of managing the Baudelaire affairs since the fire, and I must tell you that he was not doing a very good job. His two main duties were finding the orphans a good home and protecting the enormous fortune that the children's parents had left behind, and so far each home had been a catastrophe, a word which here means "an utter disaster involving tragedy, deception, and Count Olaf." Count Olaf was a terrible man who wanted the Baudelaire fortune for himself, and tried every disgusting scheme he could think of to steal it. Time after time he had come very close to succeeding, and time after time the Baudelaire orphans had revealed his plan, and time after time he had escaped—and all Mr. Poe had ever done was cough. Now he was accompanying the children to Paltryville, and it pains me to tell you that once again Count Olaf would appear with yet another disgusting scheme, and that Mr. Poe would once again fail to do anything even remotely helpful. "What a lovely forest!" Mr. Poe said again, when he was done coughing. "I think you children will have a good home here. I hope you do, anyway, because I've just received a promotion at Mulctuary Money Management. I'm now the Vice President in Charge of Coins, and from now on I will be busier than ever. If anything goes wrong with you here, I will have to send you to boarding school until I have time to find you another home, so please be on your best behavior."

"Of course, Mr. Poe," Violet said, not adding that she and her siblings had always been on their best behavior but that it hadn't done them any good.

"What is our new caretaker's name?" Klaus asked. "You haven't told us."

Mr. Poe took a piece of paper out of his pocket and squinted at it. "His name is Mr. Wuz— Mr. Qui— I can't pronounce it. It's very long and complicated."

"Can I see?" Klaus asked. "Maybe I can figure out how to pronounce it."

"No, no," Mr. Poe said, putting the paper away. "If it's too complicated for an adult, it's much too complicated for a child."

"Ghand!" Sunny shrieked. Like many infants, Sunny spoke mostly in sounds that were often difficult to translate. This time she probably meant something like "But Klaus reads many complicated books!"

"He'll tell you what to call him," Mr. Poe continued, as if Sunny had not spoken. "You'll find him at the main office of the Lucky Smells Lumbermill, which I'm told is a short walk from the train station."

"Aren't you coming with us?" Violet asked.

"No," Mr. Poe said, and coughed again into his handkerchief. "The train only stops at Paltry-ville once a day, so if I got off the train I would have to stay overnight and I'd miss another day at the bank. I'm just dropping you off here and heading right back into the city."

The Baudelaire orphans looked worriedly out the window. They weren't very happy about just being dropped off in a strange place, as if they were a pizza being delivered instead of three children all alone in the world.

"What if Count Olaf shows up?" Klaus asked quietly. "He swore he'd find us again."

"I have given Mr. Bek— Mr. Duy— I have given your new caretaker a complete descrip-tion of Count Olaf," said Mr. Poe. "So if by some stretch of the imagination he shows up

in Paltryville, Mr. Sho— Mr. Gek— will notify
the authorities."

"But Count Olaf is always in disguise,"
Violet pointed out. "It's often difficult to recognize him. Just about the only way you can tell
it's him is if you see that tattoo of an eye that he
has on his ankle."

"I included the tattoo in my description,"
Mr. Poe said impatiently.

"But what about Count Olaf's assistants?"
Klaus asked. "He usually brings at least one of
them with him, to help out with his treachery."

"I described all of them to Mr.— I have
described all of them to the owner of the mill,"
Mr. Poe said, holding a finger up as he counted
off Olaf's horrible associates. "The hook-handed
man. The bald man with the long nose. Two
women with white powder all over their faces.
And that rather chubby one who looks like
neither a man nor a woman. Your new guardian
is aware of them all, and if there's any problem,

remember you can always contact me or any of my associates at Mulctuary Money Management."

"Casca," Sunny said glumly. She probably meant something like "That's not very reassuring," but nobody heard her over the sound of the train whistle as they arrived at Paltryville Station.

"Here we are," Mr. Poe said, and before the children knew it they were standing in the station, watching the train pull away into the dark trees of the Finite Forest. The clattering noise of the train engine got softer and softer as the train raced out of sight, and soon the three siblings were all alone indeed.

"Well," Violet said, picking up the small bag that contained the children's few clothes, "let's find the Lucky Smells Lumbermill. Then we can meet our new caretaker."

"Or at least learn his name," Klaus said glumly, and took Sunny's hand.

If you are ever planning a vacation, you may

find it useful to acquire a guidebook, which is a book listing interesting and pleasant places to visit and giving helpful hints about what to do when you arrive. Paltryville is not listed in any guidebook, and as the Baudelaire orphans trudged down Paltryville's one street, they instantly saw why. There were a few small shops on either side of the street, but none of them had any windows. There was a post office, but instead of a flag flying from the flagpole, there was only an old shoe dangling from the top of it, and across from the post office was a high wooden wall that ran all the way to the end of the street. In the middle of the wall was a tall gate, also made of wood, with the words "Lucky Smells Lumbermill" written on it in letters that looked rough and slimy. Alongside the sidewalk, where a row of trees might have been, were towering stacks of old newspapers instead. In short, everything that might make a town interesting or pleasant had been made boring or unpleasant, and if Paltryville had been listed in a guidebook the only helpful hint about what to do when you got there would be: "Leave." But the three youngsters couldn't leave, of course, and with a sigh Violet led her younger siblings to the wooden gate. She was about to knock when Klaus touched her on the shoulder and said, "Look."

"I know," she said. Violet thought he was talking about the letters spelling out "Lucky Smells Lumbermill." Now that they were standing at the gate, the children could see why the letters looked rough and slimy: they were made out of wads and wads of chewed-up gum, just stuck on the gate in the shapes of letters. Other than a sign I saw once that said "Beware" in letters made of dead monkeys, the "Lucky Smells Lumbermill" sign was the most disgusting sign on earth, and Violet thought her brother was pointing that out. But when she turned to agree with him, she saw he wasn't looking at the sign, but down to the far end of the street.

"Look," Klaus said again, but Violet had

already seen what he was looking at. The two of them stood there without speaking a word, staring hard at the building at the end of Paltry-ville's one street. Sunny had been examining some of the teeth marks in the gum, but when her siblings fell silent she looked up and saw it, too. For a few seconds the Baudelaire orphans just looked.

"It must be a coincidence," Violet said, after a long pause.

"Of course," Klaus said nervously, "a coinci-dence."

"Varni," Sunny agreed, but she didn't be-lieve it. None of the orphans did. Now that the children had reached the mill, they could see another building, at the far end of the street. Like the other buildings in town, it had no win-dows, just a round door in the center. But it was the way the building was shaped, and how it was painted, that made the Baudelaires stare. The building was a sort of oval shape, with curved, skinny sticks sticking out of the top of it. Most of the oval was painted a brownish color, with a big circle of white inside the oval, and a smaller circle of green inside the white circle, and some little black steps led to a little round door that was painted black, so it looked like an even smaller circle inside the green one. The building had been made to look like an eye.

The three children looked at one another, and then at the building, and then at each other again, shaking their heads. Try as they might, they just couldn't believe it was a coincidence that the town in which they were to live had a building that looked just like the tattoo of Count Olaf.

Two

It is much, much worse to receive bad news through the written word than by somebody simply telling you, and I'm sure you understand why. When somebody simply tells you bad news, you hear it once, and that's the end of it. But when bad news is written down, whether in a letter or a newspaper or on your arm in felt tip pen, each time you read it, you feel as if you are receiving the news again and again. For instance, I once loved a woman, who for various reasons could not marry me. If she had simply told me in person, I would have been very sad, of course, but eventually it might have passed. However, she chose instead to write a two-hundred-page book, explaining every single detail of the bad news at great length, and instead my sadness has been of impossible depth. When the book was first brought to me, by a flock of carrier pigeons, I stayed up all night reading it, and I read it still, over and over, and it is as if my darling Beatrice is bringing me bad news every day and every night of my life.

The Baudelaire orphans knocked again and again on the wooden gate, taking care not to hit the chewed-up gum letters with their knuckles, but nobody answered, and at last they tried the gate themselves and found that it was unlocked. Behind the gate was a large courtyard with a dirt floor, and on the dirt floor was an envelope with the word "Baudelaires" typed on the front. Klaus picked up the envelope and opened it, and inside was a note that read as follows:

Memorandum

To: The Baudelaire Orphans

From: Lucky Smells Lumbermill

Subject: Your Arrival

Enclosed you will find a map of the Lucky Smells Lumbermill, including the dormitory where the three of you will be staying, free of charge. Please report to work the following morning along with the other employees. The owner of Lucky Smells Lumbermill expects you to be both assiduous and diligent.

"What do those words mean, 'assiduous' and 'diligent'?" Violet asked, peering over Klaus's shoulder.

"'Assiduous' and 'diligent' both mean the

same thing," said Klaus, who knew lots of impressive words from all the books he had read. "'Hardworking.'"

"But Mr. Poe didn't say anything about *working* in the the lumbermill," Violet said. "I thought we were just going to live here."

Klaus frowned at the hand-drawn map that was attached to the note with another wad of gum. "This map looks pretty easy to read," he said. "The dormitory is straight ahead, between the storage shed and the lumbermill itself."

Violet looked straight ahead and saw a gray windowless building on the other side of the courtyard. "I don't want to live," she said, "between the storage shed and the lumbermill itself."

"It doesn't sound like much fun," Klaus admitted, "but you never know. The mill might have complicated machines, and you would find it interesting to study them."

"That's true," Violet said. "You never know.

It might have some hard wood, and Sunny would find it interesting to bite it."

"Snevi!" Sunny shrieked.

"And there might be some interesting lumbermill manuals for me to read," Klaus said. "You never know."

"That's right," Violet said. "You never know. This might be a wonderful place to live."

The three siblings looked at one another, and felt a little better. It is true, of course, that you never know. A new experience can be extremely pleasurable, or extremely irritating, or somewhere in between, and you never know until you try it out. And as the children began walking toward the gray, windowless building, they felt ready to try out their new home at the Lucky Smells Lumbermill, because you never know. But—and my heart aches as I tell you this—I always know. I know because I have been to the Lucky Smells Lumbermill, and learned of all the atrocious things that befell these poor orphans during the brief time they lived there. I know because I have talked to some of the people who were there at the time, and heard with my own ears the troublesome story of the children's stay in Paltryville. And I know because I have written down all the details in order to convey to you, the reader, just how miserable their experience was. I know, and this knowledge sits in my heart, heavy as a paperweight. I wish I could have been at the lumbermill when the Baudelaires were there, because they didn't know. I wish I could tell them what I know, as they walked across the courtyard, raising small clouds of dust with every step. They didn't know, but I know and I wish they knew, if you know what I mean.

When the Baudelaires reached the door of the gray building, Klaus took another look at the map, nodded his head, and knocked. After a long pause, the door creaked open and revealed a confused-looking man whose clothes were covered in sawdust. He stared at them for quite some time before speaking.

"No one has knocked on this door," he said finally, "for fourteen years."

Sometimes, when somebody says something so strange that you don't know what to say in return, it is best to just politely say "How do you do?"

"How do you do?" Violet said politely. "I am Violet Baudelaire, and these are my siblings, Klaus and Sunny."

The confused-looking man looked even more confused, and put his hands on his hips, brushing some of the sawdust off his shirt. "Are you sure you're in the right place?" he asked.

"I think so," Klaus said. "This is the dormitory at the Lucky Smells Lumbermill, isn't it?"

"Yes," the man said, "but we're not allowed to have visitors."

"We're not visitors," Violet replied. "We're going to live here."

The man scratched his head, and the Baude-laires watched as sawdust fell out of his messy gray hair. "You're going to live *here*, at the Lucky Smells Lumbermill?"

"Cigam!" Sunny shrieked, which meant "Look at this note!"

Klaus gave the note to the man, who was careful not to touch the gum as he read it over. Then he looked down at the orphans with his tired, sawdust-sprinkled eyes. "You're going to *work* here, too? Children, working in a lumber-mill is a very difficult job. Trees have to be stripped of their bark and sawed into narrow strips to make boards. The boards have to be tied together into stacks and loaded onto trucks. I must tell you that the majority of people who work in the lumber business are grown-ups. But if the owner says you're working here, I guess you're working here. You'd better come inside."

The man opened the door further, and the Baudelaires stepped inside the dormitory. "My name's Phil, by the way," Phil said. "You can join us for dinner in a few minutes, but in the meantime I'll give you a tour of the dormitory." Phil led the youngsters into a large, dimly lit room filled with bunk beds, standing in rows and rows on a cement floor. Sitting or lying down on the bunks were an assortment of people, men and women, all of whom looked tired and all of whom were covered in sawdust. They were sitting together in groups of four or five, playing cards, chatting quietly, or simply staring into space, and a few of them looked up with mild interest as the three siblings walked into the room. The whole place had a damp smell, a smell rooms get when the windows have not been opened for quite some time. Of course, in this case the windows had never been opened, because there weren't any windows, although the children could see that somebody had taken a ballpoint pen and drawn a few windows on the gray cement walls. The window drawings somehow made the room even more pathetic, a word which here means "depressing and containing no windows," and the Baudelaire orphans felt a lump in their throats just looking at it.

"This here is the room where we sleep," Phil said. "There's a bunk over there in the far corner that you three can have. You can store your bag underneath the bed. Through that door is the bathroom and down that hallway over there is the kitchen. That's pretty much the grand tour. Everyone, this is Violet, Klaus, and Sunny. They're going to work here."

"But they're *children*," one of the women said.

"I know," Phil said. "But the owner says they're going to work here, so they're going to work here."

"By the way," Klaus said, "what is the owner's name? Nobody has told us."

"I don't know," Phil said, stroking his dusty chin. "He hasn't visited the dormitory for six years or so. Does anybody remember the owner's name?"

"I think it's Mister something," one of the men said.

"You mean you never talk to him?" Violet asked.

"We never even see him," Phil said. "The owner lives in a house across from the storage shed, and only comes to the lumbermill for special occasions. We see the foreman all the time, but never the owner."

"Teruca?" Sunny asked, which probably meant "What's a foreman?"

"A foreman," Klaus explained, "is somebody who supervises workers. Is he nice, Phil?"

"He's *awful*!" one of the other men said, and some of the others took up the cry.

"He's *terrible*!"

"He's *disgusting*!"

"He's *revolting*!"

"He's *the worst foreman the world has ever seen*!"

"He is pretty bad," Phil said to the Baudelaires. "The guy we used to have, Foreman Firstein, was O.K. But last week he stopped showing up. It was very odd. The man who replaced him, Foreman Flacutono, is very mean. You'll stay on his good side if you know what's good for you."

"He doesn't have a good side," a woman said.

"Now, now," Phil said. "Everything and everybody has a good side. Come on, let's have our supper."

The Baudelaire orphans smiled at Phil, and followed the other employees of the Lucky Smells Lumbermill into the kitchen, but they still had lumps in their throats as big as the lumps in the beef casserole that they ate for supper. The children could tell, from Phil's statement about everything and everybody having a good side, that he was an optimist. "Optimist" is a word which here refers to a person, such as Phil, who thinks hopeful and pleasant thoughts about nearly everything. For instance, if an optimist had his left arm chewed off by an alligator, he might say, in a pleasant and hopeful voice, "Well, this isn't too bad. I don't have my left arm anymore, but at least nobody will ever ask me whether I am right-handed or left-handed," but most of us would say something more along the lines of "Aaaaah! My arm! My arm!"

The Baudelaire orphans ate their damp casserole, and they tried to be optimists like Phil, but try as they might, none of their thoughts turned out pleasant or hopeful. They thought of the bunk bed they would share, in the smelly room with windows drawn on the walls. They thought of doing hard work in the lumbermill, getting sawdust all over them and being bossed around by Foreman Flacutono. They thought of the eye-shaped building out-side the wooden gate. And most of all, they thought of their parents, their poor parents whom they missed so much and whom they would never see again. They thought all through supper, and they thought while changing into their pajamas, and they thought as Violet tossed and turned in the top bunk and Klaus and

Sunny tossed and turned below her. They thought, as they did in the courtyard, that you never know, and that their new home could still be a wonderful one. But they could guess. And as the Lucky Smells employees snored around them, the children thought about all their unhappy circumstances, and began guessing. They tossed and turned, and guessed and guessed, and by the time they fell asleep there wasn't a single optimist in the Baudelaire bunk.

Three

Morning is an important time of day, because how you spend your morning can often tell you what kind of day you are going to have. For instance, if you wake up to the sound of twittering birds, and find yourself in an enormous canopy bed, with a butler standing next to you holding a breakfast of freshly made muffins and hand-squeezed orange juice on a silver tray, you will know that your day will be a splendid one. If you wake up to the sound of church bells, and find yourself in a fairly big regular bed, with a butler standing next to you holding a breakfast of hot tea and toast on a plate, you will know that your day will be O.K. And if you wake up to the sound of somebody banging two metal pots together, and find yourself in a small bunk bed, with a nasty foreman standing in the doorway holding no breakfast at all, you will know that your day will be horrid.

You and I, of course, cannot be too surprised that the Baudelaire orphans' first day at the Lucky Smells Lumbermill was a horrid one. And the Baudelaires certainly did not expect twittering birds or a butler, not after their dismaying arrival. But never in their most uneasy dreams did they expect the cacophony—a word which here means "the sound of two metal pots being banged together by a nasty foreman standing in the doorway holding no breakfast at all"—that awoke them.

"Get up, you lazy, smelly things!" cried the foreman in an odd-sounding voice. He spoke as if he were covering his mouth with his hands. "Time for work, everybody! There's a new shipment of logs just waiting to be made into lumber!"

The children sat up and rubbed their eyes. All around them, the employees of the Lucky Smells Lumbermill were stretching and covering their ears at the sound of the pots. Phil, who was already up and making his bunk neatly, gave the Baudelaires a tired smile.

"Good morning, Baudelaires," Phil said. "And good morning, Foreman Flacutono. May I introduce you to your three newest employees? Foreman Flacutono, this is Violet, Klaus, and Sunny Baudelaire."

"I heard we'd have some new workers," the foreman said, dropping the pots to the floor with a clatter, "but nobody told me they'd be midgets."

"We're not midgets," Violet explained. "We're children."

"Children, midgets, what do I care?" Foreman Flacutono said in his muffled voice, walking over to the orphans' bunk. "All I care is that you get out of bed this instant and go straight to the mill."

The Baudelaires hopped out of the bunk bed, not wanting to anger a man who banged pots together instead of saying "Good morning." But once they got a good look at Foreman Flacutono they wanted to hop back into their bunks and pull the covers over their heads.

I'm sure you have heard it said that appearance does not matter so much, and that it is what's on the inside that counts. This is, of course, utter nonsense, because if it were true then people who were good on the inside would never have to comb their hair or take a bath, and the whole world would smell even worse than it already does. Appearance matters a great deal, because you can often tell a lot about people by looking at how they present themselves. And it was the way Foreman Flacutono presented himself that made the orphans want to jump back into their bunks. He was wearing stained overalls, which never make a good impression, and his shoes were taped shut instead of being tied up with laces. But it was the foreman's head that was the most unpleasant. Foreman Flacutono was bald, as bald as an egg, but rather than admit to being bald like sensible people do, he had purchased a curly white wig that made it look like he had a bunch of large dead worms all over his head. Some of the worm hairs stuck straight up, and some of them curled off to one side, and some of them ran down his ears and his forehead, and a few of them stretched straight out ahead as if they wanted to escape from Foreman Flacutono's scalp. Below his wig was a pair of dark and beady eyes, which blinked at the orphans in a most unpleasant way.

As for the rest of his face, it was impossible to tell what it looked like, because it was covered with a cloth mask, such as doctors wear when they are in hospitals. Foreman Flacutono's nose was all curled up under the mask, like an alligator hiding in the mud, and when he spoke the Baudelaires could see his mouth opening and closing behind the cloth. It is perfectly proper to wear these masks in hospitals, of course, to stop the spreading of germs, but it makes no sense if you are the foreman of the Lucky Smells Lumbermill. The only reason Foreman Flacutono could have for wearing a surgical mask would be to frighten people, and as he peered down at the Baudelaire orphans they were quite frightened indeed.

"The first thing you can do, Baudeliars," Foreman Flacutono said, "is pick up my pots. And never make me drop them again."

"But we didn't make you drop them," Klaus said.

"Bram!" Sunny added, which probably meant something like "and our last name is Baude*laire*."

"If you don't pick up the pots *this instant*," Foreman Flacutono said, "you will get no chewing gum for lunch."

The Baudelaire orphans did not care much for chewing gum, particularly peppermint chewing gum, which they were allergic to, but they ran to the pots. Violet picked one up and Sunny picked up the other, while Klaus hurriedly made the beds.

"Give them to me," Foreman Flacutono snapped, and grabbed the pots out of the girls' hands. "Now, workers, we've wasted enough time already. To the mills! Logs are waiting for us!"

"I hate log days," one of the employees grumbled, but everyone followed Foreman Flacutono out of the dormitory and across the dirt-floored courtyard to the lumbermill, which was a dull gray building with many smokestacks sticking out of the top like a porcupine's quills. The three children looked at one another worriedly. Except for one summer day, back when their parents were still alive, when the Baudelaires had opened a lemonade stand in front of their house, the orphans had never had jobs, and they were nervous.

The Baudelaires followed Foreman Flacutono

into the lumbermill and saw that it was all one huge room, filled with enormous machines. Violet looked at a shiny steel machine with a pair of steel pinchers like the arms of a crab, and tried to figure out how this invention worked. Klaus examined a machine that looked like a big cage, with an enormous ball of string trapped inside, and tried to remember what he had read about lumbermills. Sunny stared at a rusty, creaky-looking machine that had a circular sawblade that looked quite jagged and fearsome and wondered if it was sharper than her own teeth. And all three Baudelaires gazed at a machine, covered in tiny smokestacks, that held a huge, flat stone up in the air, and wondered what in the world it was doing there.

The Baudelaires had only a few seconds to be curious about these machines, however, before Foreman Flacutono began clanging his two pots together and barking out orders. "The logs!" he shouted. "Turn on the pincher machine and get started with the logs!"

Phil ran to the pincher machine and pressed an orange button on it. With a rough whistling noise, the pinchers opened, and stretched toward the far wall of the lumbermill. The orphans had been so curious about the machines that they hadn't noticed the huge pile of trees that were stacked, leaves and roots and all, along one wall of the lumbermill as if a giant had simply torn a small forest out of the ground and dropped it into the room. The pinchers picked up the tree on top of the stack and began lowering it to the ground, while Foreman Flacutono banged his pots together and shouted, "The debarkers! The debarkers!"

Another employee walked to the back corner of the room, where there were a stack of tiny green boxes and a pile of flat metal rectangles, as long and as thin as an adult eel. Without a word she picked up the pile of rectangles and began distributing them to the workers. "Take a debarker," she whispered to the children. "One each."

The children each took a rectangle and stood there, confused and hungry, just as the tree touched the ground. Foreman Flacutono clanged his pots together again, and the employees crowded around the tree and began scraping against it with their debarkers, filing the bark off each tree as you or I might file our nails. "You, too, midgets!" the foreman shouted, and the children found room among the adults to scrape away at the tree.

Phil had described the rigors of working in a lumbermill, and it had certainly sounded difficult. But as you remember, Phil was an optimist, so the actual work turned out to be much, much worse. For one thing, the debarkers were adult-sized, and it was difficult for the children to use them. Sunny could scarcely lift her debarker at all, and so used her teeth instead, but Violet and Klaus had teeth of only an average sharpness and so had to struggle with the debarkers. The three children scraped and

scraped, but only tiny pieces of bark fell from
the tree. For another thing, the children had not
eaten any breakfast, and as the morning wore
on they were so hungry that it was difficult to
even lift the debarker, let alone scrape it against
the tree. And for one more thing, once a tree
was finally cleared of bark, the pinchers would
drop another one onto the ground, and they
would have to start all over again, which was
extremely boring. But for the worst thing of all,
the noise at the Lucky Smells Lumbermill was
simply deafening. The debarkers made their
displeasing scraping sound as they dragged
across the trees. The pinchers made their rough
whistling noise as they picked up logs. And
Foreman Flacutono made his horrendous clanging noise as he banged his pots together. The
orphans grew exhausted and frustrated. Their
stomachs hurt and their ears rang. And they
were unbelievably bored.

Finally, as the employees finished their

fourteenth log, Foreman Flacutono banged his pots together and shouted, "Lunch break!" The workers stopped scraping, and the pinchers stopped whistling, and everyone sat down, exhausted, on the ground. Foreman Flacutono threw his pots on the floor, walked over to the tiny green boxes, and grabbed one. Opening it with a rip, he began to toss small pink squares at the workers, one to each. "You have five minutes for lunch!" he shouted, throwing three pink squares at the children. The Baudelaires could see that a damp patch had appeared on his surgical mask, from spit flying out of his mouth as he gave orders. "Just five minutes!"

Violet looked from the damp patch on the mask to the pink square in her hand, and for a second she didn't believe what she was looking at. "It's gum!" she said. "This is gum!"

Klaus looked from his sister's square to his own. "Gum isn't *lunch*!" he cried. "Gum isn't even a *snack*!"

"Tanco!" Sunny shrieked, which meant

something along the lines of "And babies shouldn't even have gum, because they could choke on it!"

"You'd better eat your gum," Phil said, moving over to sit next to the children. "It's not very filling, but it's the only thing they'll let you eat until dinnertime."

"Well, maybe we can get up a little earlier tomorrow," Violet said, "and make some sandwiches."

"We don't have any sandwich-making ingredients," Phil said. "We just get one meal, usually a casserole, every evening."

"Well, maybe we can go into town and buy some ingredients," Klaus said.

"I wish we could," Phil said, "but we don't have any money."

"What about your wages?" Violet asked. "Surely you can spend some of the money you earn on sandwich ingredients."

Phil gave the children a sad smile, and reached into his pocket. "At the Lucky Smells

Lumbermill," he said, bringing out a bunch of tiny scraps of paper, "they don't pay us in money. They pay us in coupons. See, here's what we all earned yesterday: twenty percent off a shampoo at Sam's Haircutting Palace. The day before that we earned this coupon for a free refill of iced tea, and last week we earned this one: 'Buy Two Banjos and Get One Free.' The trouble is, we can't buy two banjos, because we don't have anything but these coupons."

"Nelnu!" Sunny shrieked, but Foreman Flacutono began banging his pots together before anyone could realize what she meant.

"Lunch is over!" he shouted. "Back to work, everyone! Everyone except you, Baudelamps! The boss wants to see you three in his office right away!"

The three siblings put down their debarkers and looked at one another. They had been working so hard that they had almost forgotten about meeting their guardian, whatever his name was. What sort of man would force small children to work in a lumbermill? What sort of man would hire a monster like Foreman Flacutono? What sort of man would pay his employees in coupons, or feed them only gum?

Foreman Flacutono banged his pots together again and pointed at the door, and the children stepped out of the noisy room into the quiet of the courtyard. Klaus took the map out of his pocket and pointed the way to the office. With each step, the orphans raised small clouds of dirt that matched the clouds of dread hovering over them. Their bodies ached from the morning's work, and they had an uneasy feeling in their empty stomachs. As they had guessed from the way their day began, the three children were having a bad day. But as they got closer and closer to the office, they wondered if their day was about to get even worse.

CHAPTER
Four

As I'm sure you know, whenever there is a mirror around, it is almost impossible not to take a look at yourself. Even though we all know what we look like, we all like just to look at our reflections, if only to see how we're doing. As the Baudelaire orphans waited outside the office to meet their new guardian, they looked in a mirror hanging in the hallway and they saw at once that they were not doing so well. The children looked tired and they looked hungry. Violet's hair was covered in small pieces of bark. Klaus's glasses were hanging askew, a phrase which here means "tilted to one side from leaning over logs the entire morning." And there were small pieces of wood stuck in Sunny's four teeth from using them as debarkers. Behind them, reflected in the mirror, was a painting of the seashore, which was hanging on the opposite wall, which made them feel even worse, because the seashore always made them remember that terrible, terrible day when the three siblings went to the beach and soon received the news from Mr. Poe that their parents had died. The children stared at their own reflections, and stared at the painting of the seashore behind them, and it was almost unbearable to think about everything that had happened to them since that day.

"If someone had told me," Violet said, "that

day at the beach, that before long I'd find myself living at the Lucky Smells Lumbermill, I would have said they were crazy."

"If someone had told *me*," Klaus said, "that day at the beach, that before long I'd find myself pursued by a greedy, evil man named Count Olaf, I would have said they were insane."

"Wora," Sunny said, which meant something like "If someone had told *me*, that day at the beach, that before long I'd find myself using my four teeth to scrape the bark off trees, I would have said they were psychoneurotically disturbed."

The dismayed orphans looked at their reflections, and their dismayed reflections looked back at them. For several moments, the Baudelaires stood and pondered the mysterious way their lives were going, and they were thinking so hard about it that they jumped a little when somebody spoke.

"You must be Violet, Klaus, and Sunny

Baudelaire," the somebody said, and the children turned to see a very tall man with very short hair. He was wearing a bright blue vest and holding a peach. He smiled and walked toward them, but then frowned as he drew closer. "Why, you're covered in pieces of bark," he said. "I hope you haven't been hanging around the lumbermill. That can be very dangerous for small children."

Violet looked at the peach, and wondered if she dared ask for a bite. "We've been working there all morning," she said.

The man frowned. "*Working* there?"

Klaus looked at the peach, and had to stop himself from grabbing it right out of the man's hand. "Yes," he said. "We received your instructions and went right to work. Today was a new log day."

The man scratched his head. "*Instructions?*" he asked. "What in the world are you talking about?"

Sunny looked at the peach, and it was all

she could do not to leap up and sink her teeth right into it. "Molub!" she shrieked, which must have meant something like "We're talking about the typed note that told us to go to work at the lumbermill!"

"Well, I don't understand how three people as young as yourselves were put to work in the lumbermill, but please accept my humblest apologies, and let me tell you that it will not happen again. Why, you're *children*, for goodness' sake! You will be treated as members of the family!"

The orphans looked at one another. Could it be that their horrible experiences in Paltryville were just a mistake? "You mean we don't have to debark any more logs?" Violet asked.

"Of course not," the man said. "I can't believe you were even allowed inside. Why, there are some nasty machines in there. I'm going to speak to your new guardian about it immediately."

"*You're* not our new guardian?" Klaus asked.

❊ 4 9 ❊

"Oh no," the man said. "Forgive me for not introducing myself. My name is Charles, and it's very nice to have the three of you here at Lucky Smells Lumbermill."

"It's very nice to be here," Violet lied politely.

"I find that difficult to believe," Charles said, "seeing as you've been forced to work in the mill, but let's put that behind us and have a fresh start. Would you care for a peach?"

"They've had their lunch!" came a booming voice, and the orphans whirled around and stared at the man they saw. He was quite short, shorter than Klaus, and dressed in a suit made of a very shiny dark-green material that made him look more like a reptile than a person. But what made them stare most was his face—or, rather, the cloud of smoke that was covering his face. The man was smoking a cigar, and the smoke from the cigar covered his entire head. The cloud of smoke made the Baudelaire children very curious as to what his face really looked like, and you may be curious as well, but you will have to take that curiosity to your grave, for I will tell you now, before we go any further, that the Baudelaires never saw this man's face, and neither did I, and neither will you.

"Oh, hello, sir," Charles said. "I was just meeting the Baudelaire children. Did you know they had arrived?"

"Of course I knew they arrived," the smoke-faced man said. "I'm not an idiot."

"No, of course not," Charles said. "But were you aware that they were put to work in the lumbermill? On a new log day, no less! I was just explaining to them what a terrible mistake that was."

"It wasn't a mistake," the man said. "I don't make mistakes, Charles. I'm not an idiot." He turned so the cloud of smoke faced the children. "Hello, Baudelaire orphans. I thought we should lay eyes on one another."

"Batex!" Sunny shrieked, which probably meant "But we're not laying eyes on one another!"

"I have no time to talk about that," the man said. "I see you've met Charles. He's my partner. We split everything fifty-fifty, which is a good deal. Don't you think so?"

"I guess so," Klaus said. "I don't know very much about the lumber business."

"Oh, yes," Charles said. "Of course I think it's a good deal."

"Well," the man said, "I want to give you three a good deal as well. Now, I heard about what happened to your parents, which is really too bad. And I heard all about this Count Olaf fellow, who sounds like quite a jerk, and those odd-looking people who work for him. So when Mr. Poe gave me a call, I worked out a deal. The deal is this: I will try to make sure that Count Olaf and his associates never go anywhere near you, and you will work in my lumbermill until you come of age and get all that money. Is that a fair deal?"

The Baudelaire orphans did not answer this question, because it seemed to them the answer was obvious. A fair deal, as everyone knows, is when both people give something of more or less equal value. If you were bored with playing with your chemistry set, and you gave it to your brother in exchange for his dollhouse, that would be a fair deal. If someone offered to smuggle me out of the country in her sailboat, in exchange for free tickets to an ice show, that would be a fair deal. But working for years in a lumbermill in exchange for the owner's *trying* to keep Count Olaf away is an enormously unfair deal, and the three youngsters knew it.

"Oh, sir," Charles said, smiling nervously at the Baudelaires. "You can't be serious. A lumbermill is no place for small children to work."

"Of course it is," the man said. He reached a hand up into his cloud to scratch an itch somewhere on his face. "It will teach them responsibility. It will teach them the value of work. And it will teach them how to make flat wooden boards out of trees."

"Well, you probably know best," Charles said, shrugging.

"But we could *read* about all of those things," Klaus said, "and learn about them that way."

"That's true, sir," Charles said. "They could study in the library. They seem very well behaved, and I'm sure they would cause no trouble."

"Your library!" the man said sharply. "What nonsense! Don't listen to Charles, you children. My partner has insisted that we create a library for the employees at the mill, and so I let him. But it is no substitute for hard work."

"*Please*, sir," Violet pleaded. "At least let our little sister stay in the dormitory. She's only a baby."

"I have offered you a very good deal," the man said. "As long as you stay within the gates of the Lucky Smells Lumbermill, this Count

Olaf will not come near you. In addition, I'm giving you a place to sleep, a nice hot dinner, and a stick of gum for lunch. And all you have to do in return is a few years' work. That sounds like a pretty good deal to me. Well, it was nice to meet you. Unless you have any questions, I'll be going now. My pizza is getting cold, and if there's one thing I hate it's a cold lunch."

"I have a question," Violet said, although the truth of the matter is she had many questions. Most of them began with the phrase "How can you." "How can you force small children to work in a lumbermill?" was one of them. "How can you treat us so horridly, after all we've been through?" was another. And then there was "How can you pay your employees in coupons instead of money?" and "How can you feed us only gum for lunch?" and "How can you stand to have a cloud of smoke covering your face?" But none of these seemed like questions that were proper to ask, at least not out loud. So Violet looked her new guardian right in his cloud and asked, "What is your name?"

"Never mind what my name is," the man said. "No one can pronounce it anyway. Just call me Sir."

"I'll show the children to the door, Sir," Charles said quickly, and with a wave of his hand, the owner of the Lucky Smells Lumbermill was gone. Charles waited nervously for a moment, to make sure Sir was far enough away. Then he leaned in to the children and handed them the peach. "Never mind what he said about your already having your lunch," he said. "Have this peach."

"Oh, thank you," Klaus cried, and hurriedly divided the peach among himself and his siblings, giving the biggest piece to Sunny because she hadn't even had her gum. The Baudelaire children wolfed down the peach, and under normal circumstances it would not have been polite to eat something so quickly and so noisily, particularly in front of someone they did not know very well. But these circumstances were not at all normal, so even a manners expert would excuse them for their gobbling.

"You know," Charles said, "because you seem like such nice children, and because you've worked so very hard today, I'm going to do something for you. Can you guess what it is?"

"Talk to Sir," Violet said, wiping peach juice off her chin, "and convince him that we shouldn't work in the lumbermill?"

"Well, no," Charles admitted. "That wouldn't do any good. He won't listen to me."

"But you're his partner," Klaus pointed out.

"That doesn't matter," Charles replied. "When Sir has made up his mind, he has made up his mind. I know he sometimes is a little bit mean, but you'll have to excuse him. He had a very terrible childhood. Do you understand?"

Violet looked at the painting of the seashore, and thought once again of that dreadful day at the beach. "Yes," she sighed. "I understand. I think I'm having a very terrible childhood myself."

"Well, I know what will make you feel better," Charles said, "at least a little bit. Let me show you the library before you go back to work. Then you can visit it whenever you want. Come on, it's right down the hall."

Charles led the Baudelaires down the hallway, and even though they would soon be back at work, even though they had been offered one of the least fair deals ever offered to children, the three siblings felt a little bit better. Whether it was Uncle Monty's library of reptile books, or Aunt Josephine's library of grammar books, or Justice Strauss's library of law books, or, best of all, their parents' library of all kinds of books—all burned up now, alas— libraries always made them feel a little bit better. Just knowing that they could read made the Baudelaire orphans feel as if their wretched lives could be a little brighter. At the end of a hallway was a little door, and Charles stopped at the door, smiled at the children, and opened the door.

The library was a large room, and it was filled with elegant wooden bookshelves and comfortable-looking sofas on which to sit and read. On one wall was a row of windows, which let in more than enough light for reading, and on the other wall was a row of landscape paintings, perfect for resting one's eyes. The Baudelaire children stepped inside the room and took a good look around. But they did not feel any better, not at all.

"Where are the books?" Klaus asked. "All these elegant bookshelves are empty."

"That's the only thing wrong with this library," Charles admitted. "Sir wouldn't give me any money to buy books."

"You mean there are no books at all?" Violet asked.

"Just three," Charles said, and walked to the farthest bookshelf. There, on the bottom shelf, were three books sitting all by themselves. "Without money, of course, it was difficult to acquire any books, but I did have three books donated. Sir donated his book, *The History of Lucky Smells Lumbermill*. The mayor of Paltryville donated this book, *The Paltryville Constitution*. And here's *Advanced Ocular Science*, donated by Dr. Orwell, a doctor who lives in town."

Charles held up the three books to show the Baudelaires what each one looked like, and the children stared in dismay and fear. *The History of Lucky Smells Lumbermill* had a painting of Sir on the cover, with a cloud of smoke covering his face. *The Paltryville Constitution* had a photograph of the Paltryville post office, with the old shoe dangling from the flagpole in front. But it was the cover of *Advanced Ocular Science* that made the Baudelaire children stare.

You have heard, many times I'm sure, that you should not judge a book by its cover. But just as it is difficult to believe that a man who is not a doctor wearing a surgical mask and a white wig will turn out to be a charming person, it was difficult for the children to believe that

Advanced Ocular Science was going to cause them anything but trouble. The word "ocular," you might not know, means "related to the eye," but even if you didn't know this you could figure it out from the cover. For printed on the cover was an image that the children recognized. They recognized it from their own nightmares, and from personal experience. It was an image of an eye, and the Baudelaire orphans recognized it as the mark of Count Olaf.

In the days that followed, the Baudelaire orphans had pits in their stomachs. In Sunny's case it was understandable, because when Klaus had divided up the peach, she had gotten the part with the pit. Normally, of course, one does not eat the pit part of the peach, but Sunny was very hungry, and liked to eat hard things, so the pit ended up in her stomach along with the parts of the fruit that you or I might find more suitable. But the pit in the Baudelaire stomachs was not so much from the snack that Charles had given them but from an overall feeling of doom. They were certain that Count Olaf was lurking nearby, like some predator waiting to pounce on the children while they weren't looking.

So each morning, when Foreman Flacutono clanged his pots together to wake everyone up, the Baudelaires took a good look at him to see if Count Olaf had taken his place. It would have been just like Count Olaf to put a white wig on his head and a surgical mask over his face, and snatch the Baudelaires right out of their bunk. But Foreman Flacutono always had the same dark and beady eyes, which didn't look a thing like Count Olaf's shiny ones, and he always spoke in his rough, muffled voice, which was the opposite of the smooth, snarly voice of

Count Olaf. When the children walked across the dirt-floored courtyard to the lumbermill, they took a good look at their fellow employees. It would have been just like Count Olaf to get himself hired as an employee, and snatch the orphans away while Foreman Flacutono wasn't looking. But although all the workers looked tired, and sad, and hungry, none of them looked evil, or greedy, or had such awful manners.

And as the orphans performed the backbreaking labor of the lumbermill—the word "backbreaking" here means "so difficult and tiring that it felt like the orphans' backs were breaking, even though they actually weren't"—they wondered if Count Olaf would use one of the enormous machines to somehow get his hands on their fortune. But that didn't seem to be the case, either. After a few days of tearing the bark off the trees, the debarkers were put back in their corner, and the giant pincher machine was turned off. Next, the workers had to pick up the barkless trees themselves, one by one, and hold them against the buzzing circular saw until it had sliced each tree into flat boards. The youngsters' arms were soon achy and covered in splinters from lifting all of the logs, but Count Olaf did not take advantage of their weakened arms to kidnap them. After a few days of sawing, Foreman Flacutono ordered Phil to start up the machine with the enormous ball of string inside. The machine wrapped the string around small bundles of boards, and the employees had to gather around and tie the string into very complicated knots, to hold the bundles together. The siblings' fingers were soon so sore that they could scarcely hold the coupons they were given each day, but Count Olaf did not try to force them to surrender their fortune. Day after dreary day went by, and although the children were convinced that he must be somewhere nearby, Count Olaf simply did not show up. It was very puzzling.

"It is very puzzling," Violet said one day, during their gum break. "Count Olaf is simply nowhere to be found."

"I know," Klaus said, rubbing his right thumb, which was the sorest. "That building looks like his tattoo, and so does that book cover. But Count Olaf himself hasn't shown his face."

"Elund!" Sunny said thoughtfully. She probably meant something like "It is certainly perplexing."

Violet snapped her fingers, frowning because it hurt. "I've thought of something," she said. "Klaus, you just said he hasn't shown his face. Maybe he's Sir, in disguise. We can't tell what Sir really looks like because of that cloud of smoke. Count Olaf could have dressed in a green suit and taken up smoking just to fool us."

"I thought of that, too," Klaus said. "But he's much shorter than Count Olaf, and I don't know how you can disguise yourself as a much shorter person."

"Chorn!" Sunny pointed out, which meant something like "And his voice sounds nothing like Count Olaf's."

"That's true," Violet said, and gave Sunny a

small piece of wood that was sitting on the floor. Because babies should not have gum, Sunny's older siblings gave her these small tree scraps during the lunch break. Sunny did not eat the wood, of course, but she chewed on it and pretended it was a carrot, or an apple, or a beef and cheese enchilada, all of which she loved.

"It might just be that Count Olaf hasn't found us," Klaus said. "After all, Paltryville is in the middle of nowhere. It could take him years to track us down."

"Pelli!" Sunny exclaimed, which meant something like "But that doesn't explain the eye-shaped building, or the cover of the book!"

"Those things could just be coincidence," Violet admitted. "We're so scared of Count Olaf that maybe we're just thinking we're seeing him everywhere. Maybe he won't show up. Maybe we really are safe here."

"That's the spirit," said Phil, who had been sitting near them all this time. "Look on the bright side. Lucky Smells Lumbermill might not be your favorite place, but at least there's no sign of this Olaf guy you keep talking about. This might turn out to be the most fortunate part of your lives."

"I admire your optimism," Klaus said, smiling at Phil.

"Me too," Violet said.

"Tenpa," Sunny agreed.

"That's the spirit," Phil said again, and stood up to stretch his legs. The Baudelaire orphans nodded, but looked at one another out of the corners of their eyes. It was true that Count Olaf hadn't shown up, or at least he hadn't shown up yet. But their situation was far from fortunate. They had to wake up to the clanging of pots, and be ordered around by Foreman Flacutono. They only had gum—or, in Sunny's case, imaginary enchiladas—for lunch. And worst of all, working in the lumbermill was so exhausting that they didn't have the energy to do anything else. Even though she was near complicated machines every day, Violet hadn't even thought about inventing something for a very long time. Even though Klaus was free to visit Charles's library whenever he wanted to, he hadn't even glanced at any of the three books. And even though there were plenty of hard things around to bite, Sunny hadn't closed her mouth around more than a few of them. The children missed studying reptiles with Uncle Monty. They missed living over Lake Lachrymose with Aunt Josephine. And most of all, of course, they missed living with their parents, which was where, after all, they truly belonged.

"Well," Violet said, after a pause, "we'll only have to work here for a few years. Then I will be of age, and we can use some of the Baude-laire fortune. I'd like to build an inventing studio for myself, perhaps over Lake Lachry-mose, where Aunt Josephine's house used to be, so we can always remember her."

"And I'd like to build a library," Klaus said,

"that would be open to the public. And I've always hoped that we could buy back Uncle Monty's reptile collection, and take care of all the reptiles."

"Dolc!" Sunny shrieked, which meant "And I could be a dentist!"

"What in the world does 'Dolc' mean?"

The orphans looked up and saw that Charles had come into the lumbermill. He was smiling at them and taking something out of his pocket.

"Hello, Charles," Violet said. "It's nice to see you. What have you been up to?"

"Ironing Sir's shirts," Charles answered. "He has a lot of shirts, and he's too busy to iron them himself. I've been meaning to come by, but the ironing took a long time. I brought you some beef jerky. I was afraid to take more than a little bit, because Sir would know that it was missing, but here you go."

"Thank you very much," Klaus said politely. "We'll share this with the other employees."

"Well, O.K.," Charles said, "but last week they got a coupon for thirty percent off beef jerky, so they probably bought plenty of it."

"Maybe they did," Violet said, knowing full well that there was no way any of the workers could afford beef jerky. "Charles, we've been meaning to ask you about one of the books in your library. You know the one with the eye on the cover? Where did you—"

Violet's question was interrupted by the sound of Foreman Flacutono's pots being banged together. "Back to work!" he shouted. "Back to work! We have to finish tying the bundles today, so there's no time for chitchat!"

"I would just like to talk to these children for a few more minutes, Foreman Flacutono," Charles said. "Surely we can extend the lunch break just a little bit."

"Absolutely not!" Foreman Flacutono said, striding over to the orphans. "I have my orders from Sir, and I intend to carry them out. Unless you'd like to tell Sir that—"

"Oh, no," Charles said quickly, backing away from Foreman Flacutono. "I don't think that's necessary."

"Good," the foreman said shortly. "Now get up, midgets! Lunch is over!"

The children sighed and stood up. They had long ago given up trying to convince Foreman Flacutono that they weren't midgets. They waved good-bye to Charles, and walked slowly to the waiting bundle of boards, with Foreman Flacutono walking behind them, and at that moment one of the children had a trick played on him which I hope has never been played on you. This trick involves sticking your foot out in front of a person who is walking, so the person trips and falls on the ground. A police- man did it to me once, when I was carrying a crystal ball belonging to a Gypsy fortune-teller who never forgave me for tumbling to the ground and shattering her ball into hundreds of pieces. It is a mean trick, and it is easy to do, and I'm sorry to say that Foreman Flacutono did it to Klaus right at this moment. Klaus fell right to the ground of the lumbermill, his glasses falling off his face and skittering over to the bundle of boards.

"Hey!" Klaus said. "You tripped me!"

One of the most annoying aspects of this sort of trick is that the person who does it usually pretends not to know what you're talking about. "I don't know what you're talking about," Foreman Flacutono said.

Klaus was too annoyed to argue. He stood up, and Violet walked over to fetch his glasses. But when she leaned over to pick them up, she saw at once that something was very, very wrong.

"Rotup!" Sunny shrieked, and she spoke the truth. When Klaus's glasses had skittered across the room, they had scraped against the floor and hit the boards rather hard. Violet picked the glasses up, and they looked like a piece of modern sculpture a friend of mine made long ago. The sculpture was called *Twisted, Cracked, and Hopelessly Broken*.

"My brother's glasses!" Violet cried. "They're twisted, and cracked! They're hopelessly broken, and he can scarcely see anything without them!"

"Too bad for you," Foreman Flacutono said, shrugging at Klaus.

"Oh, don't be ridiculous," Charles said. "He needs a replacement pair, Foreman Flacutono. A child could see that."

"Not me," Klaus said. "I can scarcely see anything."

"Well, take my arm," Charles said. "There's no way you can work in a lumbermill without being able to see what you're doing. I'll take you to the eye doctor right away."

"Oh, thank you," Violet said, relieved.

"Is there an eye doctor nearby?" Klaus asked.

"Oh yes," Charles replied. "The closest one is Dr. Orwell, who wrote that book you were talking about. Dr. Orwell's office is just outside the doors of the mill. I'm sure you noticed it on your way here—it's made to look like a giant eye. Come on, Klaus."

"Oh, no, Charles!" Violet said. "Don't take him there!"

Charles cupped a hand to his ear. "What did you say?" he shouted. Phil had flipped a switch on the string machine, and the ball of string had begun to spin inside its cage, making a loud whirring sound as the employees got back to work.

"That building has the mark of Count Olaf!" Klaus shouted, but Foreman Flacutono had begun to clang his pots together, and Charles shook his head to indicate he couldn't hear.

"Yoryar!" Sunny shrieked, but Charles just shrugged and led Klaus out of the mill.

The two Baudelaire sisters looked at one another. The whirring sound continued, and Foreman Flacutono kept on clanging his pots, but that wasn't the loudest sound that the two girls heard. Louder than the machine, louder than the pots, was the sound of their own furiously beating hearts as Charles took their brother away.

C H A P T E R
Six

"*I* tell you, you have nothing to worry about," Phil said, as Violet and Sunny picked at their casserole. It was dinnertime, but Klaus had still not returned from Dr. Orwell's, and the young Baudelaire women were worried sick. After work, while walking across the dirty courtyard with their fellow employees, Violet and Sunny had peered worriedly at the wooden gate that led out to Paltryville, and were dismayed to see no sign of Klaus. When they arrived at the dormitory, Violet and Sunny looked out the window to watch for him, and they were so anxious that it took them several minutes to realize that the window was not a real one, but one drawn on the blank wall with a ballpoint pen. Then they went out and sat on the doorstep, looking out at the empty courtyard, until Phil called them in to supper. And now it was getting on toward bedtime, and not only had their brother still not returned, but Phil was insisting that they had nothing to worry about.

"I think we do, Phil," Violet said. "I think we *do* have something to worry about. Klaus has been gone all afternoon, and Sunny and I are worried that something might have happened to him. Something awful."

"Becer!" Sunny agreed.

"I know that doctors can seem scary to young children," Phil said, "but doctors are your friends, and they can't hurt you."

Violet looked at Phil and saw that their conversation would go nowhere. "You're right," she said tiredly, even though he was quite wrong. As anyone who's ever been to a doctor knows, doctors are not necessarily your friends, any more than mail deliverers are your friends, or butchers are your friends, or refrigerator repair-people are your friends. A doctor is a man or woman whose job it is to make you feel better, that's all, and if you've ever had a shot you know that the statement "Doctors can't hurt you" is simply absurd. Violet and Sunny, of course, were worried that Dr. Orwell had some connection with Count Olaf, not that their brother would get a shot, but it was useless to try to explain such things to an optimist. So they merely picked at their casserole and waited for their brother until it was time for bed.

"Dr. Orwell must have fallen behind in his appointments," Phil said, as Violet and Sunny tucked themselves into the bottom bunk. "His waiting room must be absolutely full."

"Suski," Sunny said sadly, which meant something along the lines of "I hope so, Phil."

Phil smiled at the two Baudelaires and turned out the lights in the dormitory. The employees whispered to each other for a few minutes, and then were quiet, and before too long Violet and Sunny were surrounded by the sound of snores. The children did not sleep, of course, but stared out into the dark room with a growing feeling of dismay. Sunny made a squeaky, sad noise, like the closing of a door, and Violet took her sister's fingers, which were sore from tying knots all day long, and blew on them gently. But even as the Baudelaire fingers felt better, the Baudelaire sisters did not. They lay together on the bunk and tried to imagine where Klaus could be and what was happening to him. But one of the worst things about Count Olaf is that his evil ways are so despicable that it is impossible to imagine what would be up his sleeve next. Count Olaf had done so many horrible deeds, all to get his hands on the Baudelaire fortune, that Violet and Sunny could scarcely bear to think what might be happening to their brother. The evening grew later and later, and the two siblings began to imagine more and more terrible things that could be happening to Klaus while they lay helpless in the dormitory.

"Stintamcunu," Sunny whispered finally, and Violet nodded. They had to go and look for him.

The expression "quiet as mice" is a puzzling one, because mice can often be very noisy, so people who are being quiet as mice may in fact be squeaking and scrambling around. The expression "quiet as mimes" is more appropriate, because mimes are people who perform theatrical routines without making a sound. Mimes are annoying and embarrassing, but they are much quieter than mice, so "quiet as mimes" is a more proper way to describe how Violet and Sunny got up from their bunk, tiptoed across the dormitory, and walked out into the night.

There was a full moon that night, and the children gazed for a moment at the quiet courtyard. The moonlight made the dirt floor look as strange and eerie as the surface of the moon. Violet picked Sunny up, and the two of them crossed the courtyard toward the heavy wooden gate leading out of the lumbermill. The only sound was the soft shuffling of Violet's feet. The orphans could not remember when they had been in a place that felt so quiet and still, which is why the sudden creaking sound made them jump in surprise. The creaking sound was as noisy as mice, and seemed to be coming from straight ahead. Violet and Sunny stared out into the gloom, and with another creak the wooden gate swung open and revealed the short figure of a person, walking slowly toward them.

"Klaus!" Sunny said, for one of the few regular words she used was the name of her brother. And to her relief, Violet saw that it was indeed Klaus who was walking toward them. He had on a new pair of glasses that looked just like his old ones, except they were so new that they shone in the moonlight. He gave his sisters a dazed and distant smile, as if they were people he did not know so well.

"Klaus, we were so worried about you," Violet said, hugging her brother as he reached them. "You were gone for so long. Whatever happened to you?"

"I don't know," Klaus said, so quietly that his sisters had to lean forward to hear him. "I can't remember."

"Did you see Count Olaf?" Violet asked. "Was Dr. Orwell working with him? Did they do anything to you?"

"I don't know," Klaus said, shaking his head. "I remember breaking my glasses, and I remember Charles taking me to the eye-shaped building. But I don't remember anything else. I scarcely remember where I am right now."

"*Klaus,*" Violet said firmly, "you are at the Lucky Smells Lumbermill in Paltryville. Surely you remember that."

Klaus did not answer. He merely looked at his sisters with wide, wide eyes, as if they were an interesting aquarium or a parade.

"Klaus?" Violet asked. "I said, *you are at the Lucky Smells Lumbermill.*"

Klaus still did not answer.

"He must be very tired," Violet said to Sunny.

"Libu," Sunny said doubtfully.

"You'd better get to bed, Klaus," Violet said. "Follow me."

At last, Klaus spoke. "Yes, sir," he said, quietly.

"*Sir?*" Violet repeated. "I'm not a sir—I'm your sister!"

But Klaus was silent once more, and Violet gave up. Still carrying Sunny, she walked back toward the dormitory, and Klaus shuffled behind her. The moon shone on his new glasses, and his steps made little clouds of dirt, but he didn't say a word. Quiet as mimes, the

Baudelaires walked back into the dormitory and tiptoed to their bunk bed. But when they reached it, Klaus merely stood nearby and stared at his two siblings, as if he had forgotten how to go to bed.

"Lie down, Klaus," Violet said gently.

"Yes, sir," Klaus replied, and lay down on the bottom bunk, still staring at his sisters. Violet sat on the edge of the bunk and removed Klaus's shoes, which he had forgotten to take off, but it seemed that he did not even notice.

"We'll discuss things in the morning," Violet whispered. "In the meantime, Klaus, try to get some sleep."

"Yes, sir," Klaus said, and immediately shut his eyes. In a second he was fast asleep. Violet and Sunny watched the way his mouth quivered, just as it had always done when he was asleep, ever since he was a tiny baby. It was a relief to have Klaus back with them, of course, but the Baudelaire sisters did not feel relieved, not one bit. They had never seen their brother act so strangely. For the rest of the night, Violet and Sunny huddled together on the top bunk, peering down and watching Klaus sleep. No matter how much they looked at him, it still felt like their brother had not returned.

CHAPTER Seven

If you have ever had a miserable experience,
then you have probably had it said to you that
you would feel better in the morning. This,
of course, is utter nonsense, because a miserable experience remains a miserable experience
even on the loveliest of mornings. For instance,
if it were your birthday, and a wart-removal
cream was the only present
you received, someone
might tell you to
get a good night's
sleep and wait
until morning,

but in the morning the tube of wart-removal cream would still be sitting there next to your uneaten birthday cake, and you would feel as miserable as ever. My chauffeur once told me that I would feel better in the morning, but when I woke up the two of us were still on a tiny island surrounded by man-eating crocodiles, and, as I'm sure you can undersand, I didn't feel any better about it.

And so it was with the Baudelaire orphans. As soon as Foreman Flacutono began clanging his pots together, Klaus opened his eyes and asked where in the world he was, and Violet and Sunny did not feel better at all.

"What is wrong with you, Klaus?" Violet asked.

Klaus looked at Violet carefully, as if they had met once, years ago, and he had forgotten her name. "I don't know," he said. "I'm having trouble remembering things. What happened yesterday?"

"That's what we want to ask you, Klaus,"

Violet said, but she was interrupted by their rude employer.

"Get up, you lazy midgets!" Foreman Flacutono shouted, walking over to the Baude-laire bunk and clanging his pots together again. "The Lucky Smells Lumbermill has no time for dawdling! Get out of bed this instant and go straight to work!"

Klaus's eyes grew very wide, and he sat up in bed. In an instant he was walking toward the door of the dormitory, without a word to his sisters.

"That's the spirit!" Foreman Flacutono said, and clanged his pots together again. "Now everybody! On to the lumbermill!"

Violet and Sunny looked at one another and hurried to follow their brother and the other employees, but Violet took one step, and some-thing made her stop. On the floor next to the Baudelaire bunk were Klaus's shoes, which she had removed the night before. Klaus had not even put them on before walking outside.

"His shoes!" Violet said, picking them up. "Klaus, you forgot your shoes!" She ran after him, but Klaus did not even look back. By the time Violet reached the door, her brother was walking barefoot across the courtyard.

"Grummle?" Sunny called after him, but he did not answer.

"Come on, children," Phil said. "Let's hurry to the lumbermill."

"Phil, there's something wrong with my brother," Violet said, watching Klaus open the door of the lumbermill and lead the other employees inside. "He scarcely says a word to us, he doesn't seem to remember anything, and look! He didn't put on his shoes this morning!"

"Well, look on the bright side," Phil said. "We're supposed to finish tying today, and next we do the stamping. Stamping is the easiest part of the lumber business."

"I don't *care* about the lumber business!" Violet cried. "Something is wrong with Klaus!"

"Let's not make trouble, Violet," Phil said, and walked off toward the lumbermill. Violet and Sunny looked at one another helplessly. They had no choice but to follow Phil across the courtyard and into the mill. Inside, the string machine was already whirring, and the employees were beginning to tie up the last few batches of boards. Violet and Sunny hurried to get a place next to Klaus, and for the next few hours they tied knots and tried to talk to their brother. But it was difficult to speak to him over the whirring of the string machine and the clanging of Foreman Flacutono's pots, and Klaus never answered them. Finally, the last pile of boards was tied together, and Phil turned off the string machine, and everybody received their gum. Violet and Sunny each grabbed one of Klaus's arms and dragged their barefooted brother to a corner of the mill to talk to him.

"Klaus, Klaus, *please* talk to me," Violet cried. "You're frightening us. You've got to tell us what Dr. Orwell did, so we can help you."

Klaus simply stared at his sister with widened eyes.

"Eshan!" Sunny shrieked.

Klaus did not say a word. He did not even put his gum into his mouth. Violet and Sunny sat down beside him, confused and frightened, and put their arms around their brother as though they were afraid he was floating away. They sat there like that, a heap of Baudelaires, until Foreman Flacutono clanged his pots together to signal the end of the break.

"Stamping time!" Foreman Flacutono said, pushing his stringy white wig out of his eyes. "Everybody line up for stamping. And *you*," he said, pointing to Klaus. "*You*, you lucky midget, will be operating the machine. Come over here so I can give you instructions."

"Yes, sir," Klaus said, in a quiet voice, and his sisters gasped in surprise. It was the first time he had spoken since they were in the dormitory. Without another word he stood up, disentangled himself from his siblings, and walked toward Foreman Flacutono while his sisters looked on amazedly.

Violet turned to her baby sister and brushed a small scrap of string out of her hair, something her mother used to do all the time. The eldest Baudelaire remembered, as she had remembered so many times, the promise she had made to her parents when Sunny was born. "You are the eldest Baudelaire child," her parents had said. "And as the eldest, it will always be your responsibility to look after your younger siblings. Promise us that you will always watch out for them and make sure they don't get into trouble." Violet knew, of course, that her parents had never guessed, when they told her this, that the sort of trouble her siblings would get into would be so ostentatiously—a word which here means "really, really"— horrendous, but still she felt as if she had let her parents down. Klaus was clearly in trouble, and Violet could not shake the feeling that it was her responsibility to get him out of it.

Foreman Flacutono whispered something to Klaus, who walked slowly over to the machine covered in smokestacks and began to operate its controls. Foreman Flacutono nodded to Klaus and clanged his pots together again. "Let the stamping begin!" he said, in his terrible muffled voice. The Baudelaires had no idea what Foreman Flacutono meant by stamping, and thought maybe it involved jumping up and down on the boards for some reason, like stamping on ants. But it turned out to be more like stamping a library book. The workers would lift a bundle of boards and place it on a special mat, and the machine would bring its huge, flat stone down on top of the boards with a thunderous *stamp!*, leaving a label in red ink that said "Lucky Smells Lumbermill." Then everyone had to blow on the stamp so it dried quickly. Violet and Sunny couldn't help wondering if people who would make their houses out of these boards would mind having the name of the lumbermill written on the walls of their homes. But, more important, they couldn't help wondering how Klaus knew how to work the stamping machine, and why Foreman Flacutono was having their brother at the controls, instead of Phil or one of the other employees.

"You see?" Phil told the Baudelaire sisters, from across a bundle of boards. "There's nothing wrong with Klaus. He's working the machine perfectly. You spent all that time worrying for nothing."

Stamp!

"Maybe," Violet said doubtfully, blowing on the M in "Lumbermill."

"And I told you that stamping was the easiest part of the lumbermill industry," Phil said. *Stamp!* "Your lips get a little sore from all the blowing, but that's all."

"Wiro," Sunny said, which meant something like "That's true, but I'm still worried about Klaus."

"That's the spirit," said Phil, misunder-
standing her. "I told you that if you just looked on
the bright side—"

Stam—crash—aah!

Phil fell to the floor in midsentence, his face
pale and sweaty. Of all the terrible noises to be
heard at the Lucky Smells Lumbermill, this one
was the most terrible by far. The thunderous
*stamp!*ing sound had been cut off by a wrench-
ing crash and a piercing shriek. The stamping
machine had gone horribly wrong, and the huge
flat stone had not been brought down where
it was supposed to be brought down, on the
bundle of boards. Most of the stone had been
brought down on the string machine, which was
now hopelessly smashed. But part of it had been
brought down on Phil's leg.

Foreman Flacutono dropped his pots and ran
over to the controls of the stamping machine,
pushing the dazed Klaus aside. With a flip of
the switch he brought the stone up again, and
everyone gathered around to see the damage.

The cage part of the string machine was split open like an egg, and the string had become completely entwined and entangled. And I simply cannot describe the grotesque and unnerving sight—the words "grotesque" and "unnerving" here mean "twisted, tangled, stained, and gory"—of poor Phil's leg. It made Violet's and Sunny's stomachs turn to gaze upon it, but Phil looked up and gave them a weak smile.

"Well," he said, "this isn't too bad. My left leg is broken, but at least I'm right-legged. That's pretty fortunate."

"Gee," one of the other employees murmured. "I thought he'd say something more along the lines of 'Aaaaah! My leg! My leg!'"

"If someone could just help me get to my foot," Phil said, "I'm sure that I can get back to work."

"Don't be ridiculous," Violet said. "You need to go to a hospital."

"Yes, Phil," another worker said. "We have those coupons from last month, fifty percent off a cast at the Ahab Memorial Hospital. Two of us will chip in and get your leg all fixed up. I'll call for an ambulance right away."

Phil smiled. "That's very kind of you," he said.

"This is a disaster!" Foreman Flacutono shouted. "This is the worst accident in the history of the lumbermill!"

"No, no," Phil said. "It's fine. I've never liked my left leg so much, anyway."

"Not your leg, you overgrown midget," Foreman Flacutono said impatiently. "The string machine! Those cost an inordinate amount of money!"

"What does 'inordinate' mean?" somebody asked.

"It means many things," Klaus said suddenly, blinking. "It can mean 'irregular.' It can mean 'immoderate.' It can mean 'disorderly.' But in the case of money, it is more likely to mean 'excessive.' Foreman Flacutono means that the string machine costs a lot of money."

The two Baudelaire sisters looked at one another and almost laughed in relief. "Klaus!" Violet cried. "You're defining things!"

Klaus looked at his sisters and gave them a sleepy smile. "I guess I am," he said.

"Nojeemoo!" Sunny shrieked, which meant something along the lines of "You appear to be back to normal," and she was right. Klaus blinked again, and then looked at the mess he had caused.

"What happened here?" he asked, frowning. "Phil, what happened to your leg?"

"It's perfectly all right," Phil said, wincing in pain as he tried to move. "It's just a little sore."

"You mean you don't remember what happened?" Violet asked.

"What happened *when*?" Klaus asked, frowning. "Why, look! I'm not wearing any shoes!"

"Well, *I* certainly remember what happened!" Foreman Flacutono shouted, pointing at Klaus. "You smashed our machine! I will tell

Sir about this right away! You've put a complete halt to the stamping process! Nobody will earn a single coupon today!"

"That's not fair!" Violet said. "It was an *accident*! And Klaus never should have been put in charge of that machine! He didn't know how to use it!"

"Well, he'd better learn," Foreman Flacutono said. "Now pick up my pots, Klaus!"

Klaus went over to pick up the pots, but halfway there Foreman Flacutono stuck his foot out, playing the same trick he had played the previous day, and I'm sorry to tell you that it worked just as well. Again, Klaus fell right to the ground of the lumbermill, and again, his glasses fell off his face and skittered over to the bundle of boards, and worst of all, once again they became all twisted and cracked and hopelessly broken, like my friend Tatiana's sculptures.

"My glasses!" Klaus cried. "My glasses are broken again!"

Violet got a funny feeling in her stomach, all quivery and slithery as if she had eaten snakes, rather than gum, during the lunch break. "Are you sure?" she asked Klaus. "Are you sure you can't wear them?"

"I'm sure," Klaus said miserably, holding them up for Violet to see.

"Well, well, well," Foreman Flacutono said. "How careless of you. I guess you're due for another appointment with Dr. Orwell."

"We don't want to bother him," Violet said quickly. "If you give me some basic supplies, I'm sure I can build some glasses myself."

"No, no," the foreman said, his surgical mask curling into a frown. "You'd better leave optometry to the experts. Say good-bye to your brother."

"Oh, no," Violet said, desperately. She thought again of the promise she made to her parents. "We'll take him! Sunny and I will bring him to Dr. Orwell."

"Derix!" Sunny shrieked, which clearly

meant something along the lines of "If we can't prevent him from going to Dr. Orwell, at least we can go with him!"

"Well, all right," said Foreman Flacutono, and his beady little eyes grew even darker than usual. "That's a good idea, come to think of it. Why don't all three of you go see Dr. Orwell?"

Eight

The Baudelaire orphans stood outside the gates of the Lucky Smells Lumbermill and looked at an ambulance rushing past them as it took Phil to the hospital. They looked at the chewed-up gum letters of the lumbermill sign. And they looked down at the cracked pavement of Paltryville's street. In short, they looked everywhere but at the eye-shaped building.

"We don't have to go," Violet said. "We could run away. We could hide until the next train arrived, and take it as far as possible. We know how to work in a lumbermill now, so we could get jobs in some other town."

"But what if he found us?" Klaus said, squinting at his sister. "Who would protect us from Count Olaf, if we were all by ourselves?"

"We could protect ourselves," Violet replied.

"How can we protect ourselves," Klaus asked, "when one of us is a baby and another one can barely see?"

"We've protected ourselves before," Violet said.

"Just barely," Klaus replied. "We've just barely escaped from Count Olaf each time. We can't run away and try to get along by ourselves, without glasses. We have to go see Dr. Orwell and hope for the best."

Sunny gave a little shriek of fear. Violet, of course, was too old to shriek except in emergency situations, but she was not too old to be frightened. "We don't know what will happen to us inside there," she said, looking at the black door in the eye's pupil. "*Think*, Klaus. Try to *think*. What happened to you when you went inside?"

"I don't know," Klaus said miserably. "I remember trying to tell Charles not to take me to the eye doctor, but he kept telling me that doctors were my friends, and not to be frightened."

"Ha!" Sunny shrieked, which meant "Ha!"

"And then what do you remember?" Violet asked.

Klaus closed his eyes in thought. "I wish I could tell you. But it's like that part of my brain has been wiped clean. It's like I was asleep from the moment I walked into that building until right there at the lumbermill."

"But you weren't asleep," Violet said. "You were walking around like a zombie. And then you caused that accident and hurt poor Phil."

"But I don't remember those things," Klaus said. "It's as if I . . ." His voice trailed off and he stared into space for a moment.

"Klaus?" Violet asked worriedly.

". . . It's as if I were hypnotized," Klaus finished. He looked at Violet and then at Sunny, and his sisters could see that he was figuring something out. "Of course. Hypnosis would explain everything."

"I thought hypnosis was only in scary movies," Violet said.

"Oh, no," Klaus answered. "I read the *Encyclopedia Hypnotica* just last year. It described all these famous cases of hypnosis throughout history. There was an ancient Egyptian king who was hypnotized. All the hypnotist had to do was shout 'Ramses!' and the king would perform chicken imitations, even though he was in front of the royal court."

"That's very interesting," Violet said, "but—"

"A Chinese merchant who lived during the Ling Dynasty was hypnotized. All the hypnotist had to do was shout 'Mao!' and the merchant would play the violin, even though he had never seen one before."

"These are amazing stories," Violet said, "but—"

"A man who lived in England in the nine-teen twenties was hypnotized. All the hypnotist had to do was shout 'Bloomsbury!' and he sud-denly became a brilliant writer, even though he couldn't read."

"Mazée!" Sunny shrieked, which probably meant "We don't have time to hear all these stories, Klaus!"

Klaus grinned. "I'm sorry," he said, "but it was a very interesting book, and I'm so pleased that it's coming in handy."

"Well, what did the book say about how to stop yourself from being hypnotized?" Violet asked.

Klaus's grin faded. "Nothing," he said.

"Nothing?" Violet repeated. "An entire en-cyclopedia about hypnosis said nothing about it at all?"

"If it did, I didn't read any of it. I thought the parts about the famous hypnosis cases were the most interesting, so I read those, but I skipped some of the boring parts."

For the first time since they had walked out of the gates of the lumbermill, the Baudelaire orphans looked at the eye-shaped building, and the building looked back at them. To Klaus, of course, Dr. Orwell's office just looked like a big blur, but to his sisters it looked like trouble. The round door, painted black to resemble the pupil of the eye, looked like a deep and endless hole, and the children felt as if they were going to fall into it.

"I'm never skipping the boring parts of a book again," Klaus said, and walked cautiously toward the building.

"You're not going inside?" Violet said incredulously, a word which here means "in a tone of voice to indicate Klaus was being foolish."

"What else can we do?" Klaus said quietly. He began to feel along the side of the building to find the door, and at this point in the story of the Baudelaire orphans, I would like to interrupt for a moment and answer a question I'm sure you are asking yourself. It is an important question, one which many, many people have asked many, many times, in many, many places all over the world. The Baudelaire orphans have asked it, of course. Mr. Poe has asked it. I have asked it. My beloved Beatrice, before her untimely death, asked it, although she asked it too late. The question is: *Where is Count Olaf?*

If you have been following the story of these three orphans since the very beginning, then you know that Count Olaf is always lurking around these poor children, plotting and scheming to get his hands on the Baudelaire fortune. Within days of the orphans' arrival at a new place, Count Olaf and his nefarious assistants—the word "nefarious" here means "Baudelaire-hating"—are usually on the scene, sneaking around and committing dastardly deeds. And yet so far he has been nowhere to be found. So, as the three youngsters reluctantly head toward Dr. Orwell's office, I know you must be asking yourself where in the world this despicable villain can be. The answer is: *Very nearby*.

Violet and Sunny walked to the eye-shaped
building and helped their brother up the steps
to the door, but before they could open it, the
pupil swung open to reveal a person in a long
white coat with a name tag reading "Dr. Orwell."
Dr. Orwell was a tall woman with blond hair
pulled back from her head and fashioned into
a tight, tight bun. She had big black boots on
her feet, and was holding a long black cane with
a shiny red jewel on the top.

"Why hello, Klaus," Dr. Orwell said, nodding formally at the Baudelaires. "I didn't
expect to see you back so soon. Don't tell me
you broke your glasses again."

"Unfortunately, yes," Klaus said.

"That's too bad," Dr. Orwell said. "But
you're in luck. We have very few appointments
today, so come on in and I'll do all the necessary tests."

The Baudelaire orphans looked at one
another nervously. This wasn't what they had
expected at all. They expected Dr. Orwell to be

a much more sinister figure—Counf Olaf in disguise, for instance, or one of his terrifying associates. They expected that they would be snatched inside the eye-shaped building, and perhaps never return. Instead Dr. Orwell was a professional-looking woman who was politely inviting them inside.

"Come on," she said, showing the way with her black cane. "Shirley, my receptionist, made some cookies that you girls can eat in the waiting room while I make Klaus's glasses. It won't take nearly as long as it did yesterday."

"Will Klaus be hypnotized?" Violet demanded.

"Hypnotized?" Dr. Orwell repeated, smiling. "Goodness, no. Hypnosis is only in scary movies."

The children, of course, knew this was not true, but they figured if Dr. Orwell thought it was true then she probably wasn't a hypnotist. Cautiously, they stepped inside the eye-shaped building and followed Dr. Orwell down a hallway decorated with medical certificates.

"This way to the office," she said. "Klaus tells me he's quite a reader. Do you two read as well?"

"Oh yes," Violet said. She was beginning to relax. "We read whenever we can."

"Have you ever encountered," Dr. Orwell said, "in your reading, the expression 'You catch more flies with honey than with vinegar'?"

"Tuzmo," Sunny replied, which meant something along the lines of "I don't believe so."

"I haven't read too many books about flies," Violet admitted.

"Well, the expression doesn't really have to do with flies," Dr. Orwell explained. "It's just a fancy way of saying that you're more likely to get what you want by acting in a sweet way, like honey, rather than in a distasteful way, like vinegar."

"That's interesting," Klaus said, wondering why Dr. Orwell was bringing it up.

"I suppose you're wondering why I'm

bringing it up," Dr. Orwell said, pausing in front of a door marked "Waiting Room." "But I think all will be clear to you in just a moment. Now, Klaus, follow me to the office, and you girls can wait in the waiting room through this door."

The children hesitated.

"It will just be a few moments," Dr. Orwell said, and patted Sunny on the head.

"Well, all right," Violet said, and gave her brother a wave as he followed the optometrist farther down the hallway. Violet and Sunny gave the door a push and went inside the waiting room, and saw in an instant that Dr. Orwell was right. All was clear to them in a moment. The waiting room was a small one, and it looked like most waiting rooms. It had a sofa and a few chairs and a small table with old magazines stacked on it, and a receptionist sitting at a desk, just like waiting rooms that you or I have been in. But when Violet and Sunny looked at the receptionist, they saw something that I hope you have never seen in a waiting room. A nameplate on the desk read "Shirley," but this was no Shirley, even though the receptionist was wearing a pale-brown dress and sensible beige shoes. For above the pale lipstick on Shirley's face, and below the blond wig on Shirley's head, was a pair of shiny, shiny eyes that the two children recognized at once. Dr. Orwell, in behaving politely, had been the honey, instead of the vinegar. The children, unfortunately, were the flies. And Count Olaf, sitting at the receptionist's desk with an evil smile, had caught them at last.

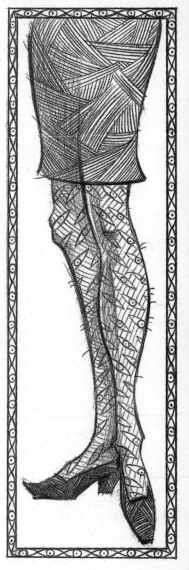

CHAPTER Nine

Oftentimes, when children are in trouble, you will hear people say that it is all because of low self-esteem. "Low self-esteem" is a phrase which here describes children who do not think much of themselves. They might think that they are ugly, or boring, or unable to do anything correctly, or some combination of these things, and whether or not they are right, you can see why those sorts of feelings might lead one into trouble. In the vast majority of cases, however, getting into trouble has nothing to do with one's self-esteem. It usually has much more to do with whatever is causing the trouble—a monster, a bus driver, a banana peel, killer bees, the school principal—than what you think of yourself.

And so it was as Violet and Sunny Baudelaire stared at Count Olaf—or, as the nameplate on his desk said, Shirley. Violet and Sunny had a very healthy amount of self-esteem. Violet knew she could do things correctly, because she had invented many devices that worked perfectly. Sunny knew she wasn't boring, because her siblings always took an interest in what she had to say. And both Baudelaire sisters knew that they weren't ugly, because they could see their pleasant facial features reflected back at them, in the middle of Count Olaf's shiny, shiny eyes. But it did not matter that they thought these things, because they were trapped.

"Why, hello there, little girls," Count Olaf said in a ridiculously high voice, as if he were really a receptionist named Shirley instead of an evil man after the Baudelaire fortune. "What are your names?"

"You *know* our names," Violet said curtly, a word which here means "tired of Count Olaf's nonsense." "That wig and that lipstick don't fool us any more than your pale-brown dress and sensible beige shoes. You're Count Olaf."

"I'm afraid you're mistaken," Count Olaf said. "I'm Shirley. See this nameplate?"

"Fiti!" Sunny shrieked, which meant "That nameplate doesn't prove anything, of course!"

"Sunny's right," Violet said. "You're not Shirley just because you have a small piece of wood with your name on it."

"I'll tell you why I'm Shirley," Count Olaf said. "I'm Shirley because I would like to be called Shirley, and it is impolite not to do so."

"I don't care if we're impolite," Violet said, "to such a disgusting person as yourself."

Count Olaf shook his head. "But if you do something impolite to *me*," he said, "then *I* might do something impolite to *you*, like for instance tearing your hair out with my bare hands."

Violet and Sunny looked at Count Olaf's hands. They noticed for the first time that he had grown his fingernails very long, and painted them bright pink as part of his disguise. The Baudelaire sisters looked at one another. Count Olaf's nails looked very sharp indeed.

"O.K., *Shirley*," Violet said. "You've been lurking around Paltryville since we arrived, haven't you?"

Shirley lifted a hand to pat her wig into place. "Maybe," she said, still in her foolish high voice.

"And you've been hiding out in the eye-shaped building this whole time, haven't you?" Violet said.

Shirley batted her eyes, and Violet and Sunny noticed that beneath her one long eyebrow—another identifying mark of Count Olaf—she was wearing long false eyelashes. "Perhaps," she said.

"And you're in cahoots with Dr. Orwell!" Violet said, using a phrase which here means "working with, in order to capture the Baudelaire fortune." "Aren't you?"

"Possibly," Shirley said, crossing her legs and revealing long white stockings imprinted with the pattern of an eye.

"Popinsh!" Sunny shrieked.

"Sunny means," Violet said, "that Dr. Orwell hypnotized Klaus and caused that terrible accident, didn't she?"

"Conceivably," Shirley said.

"And he's being hypnotized again, right now, isn't he?" Violet asked.

"It's within the bounds of the imagination," Shirley said.

Violet and Sunny looked at one another, their hearts pounding. Violet took her sister's hand and took a step backward, toward the door. "And now," she said, "you're going to try to whisk us away, aren't you?"

"Of course not," Shirley said. "I'm going

to offer you a cookie, like a good little receptionist."

"You're not a receptionist!" Violet cried.

"I certainly am," Shirley said. "I'm a poor
receptionist who lives all by herself, and who
wants very much to raise children of her own.
Three children, in fact: a smartypants little girl,
a hypnotized little boy, and a buck-toothed
baby."

"Well, you can't raise us," Violet said.
"We're already being raised by Sir."

"Oh, he'll hand you over to me soon enough,"
Shirley said, her eyes shining brightly.

"Don't be ab—" Violet said, but she stopped
herself before she could say "surd." She wanted
to say "surd." She wanted to say "Sir wouldn't
do a thing like that," but inside she wasn't so
sure. Sir had already made the three Baudelaires
sleep in one small bunk bed. He had already
made them work in a lumbermill. And he had
already only fed them gum for lunch. And as
much as she wanted to believe that it was

absurd to think that he would simply hand the Baudelaire orphans over to Shirley, Violet was not certain. She was only half sure, and so she stopped herself after half a word.

"Ab?" said a voice behind her. "What in the world does the word 'ab' mean?"

Violet and Sunny turned around and saw Dr. Orwell leading Klaus into the waiting room. He was wearing another new pair of glasses and was looking confused.

"Klaus!" Violet cried. "We were so worried ab—" She stopped herself before she could say "out" when she saw her brother's expression. It was the same expression he'd had the previous night, when he finally came back from his first appointment with Dr. Orwell. Behind his newest pair of glasses, Klaus had wide, wide eyes, and a dazed and distant smile, as if his sisters were people he did not know so well.

"There you go again, with 'ab,'" Dr. Orwell said. "Whatever in the world does it mean?"

"'Ab' isn't a word, of course," Shirley said.

"Only a stupid person would say a word like 'ab.'"

"They are stupid, aren't they?" Dr. Orwell agreed, as though they were talking about the weather instead of insulting young children. "They must have very low self-esteem."

"I couldn't agree more, Dr. Orwell," Shirley said.

"Call me Georgina," the horrible optometrist replied, winking. "Now, girls, here is your brother. He's a little tired after his appointment, but he'll be fine by tomorrow morning. More than fine, in fact. *Much* more." She turned and pointed at the door with her jeweled cane. "I believe you three know the way out."

"I don't," Klaus said faintly. "I can't remember coming in here."

"That often happens after optometry appointments," Dr. Orwell said smoothly. "Now run along, orphans."

Violet took her brother by the hand and

began to lead him out of the waiting room. "We're really free to go?" she asked, not believing it for a moment.

"Of course," Dr. Orwell said. "But I'm sure my receptionist and I will see you soon. After all, Klaus seems to have gotten very clumsy lately. He's always causing accidents."

"Roopish!" Sunny shrieked. She probably meant "They're not accidents! They're the results of hypnotism!" but the adults paid no attention. Dr. Orwell merely stepped out of the doorway and Shirley wiggled her pink fingers at them in a scrawny wave.

"Toodle-oo, orphans!" Shirley said. Klaus looked at Shirley and waved back as Violet and Sunny led him by the hand out of the waiting room.

"How could you wave to her?" Violet hissed to her brother, as they walked back down the hallway.

"She seems like a nice lady," Klaus said,

frowning. "I know I've met her somewhere before."

"Ballywot!" Sunny shrieked, which undoubtedly meant "She's Count Olaf in disguise!"

"If you say so," Klaus said vaguely.

"Oh, Klaus," Violet said miserably. "Sunny and I wasted time arguing with Shirley when we should have been rescuing you. You've been hypnotized again; I know it. Try to concentrate, Klaus. Try to remember what happened."

"I broke my glasses," Klaus said slowly, "and then we left the lumbermill. . . . I'm very tired, Veronica. Can I go to bed?"

"*Violet,*" Violet said. "My name is *Violet,* not Veronica."

"I'm sorry," Klaus said. "I'm just so tired."

Violet opened the door of the building, and the three orphans stepped out onto the depressing street of Paltryville. Violet and Sunny stopped and remembered when they had first reached the lumbermill after getting off the train, and had seen the eye-shaped building.

Their instincts had told them that the building was trouble, but the children had not listened to their instincts. They had listened to Mr. Poe.

"We'd better take him to the dormitory," Violet said to Sunny. "I don't know what else we can do with Klaus in this state. Then we should tell Sir what has happened. I hope he can help us."

"Guree," Sunny agreed glumly. The sisters led their brother through the wooden gates of the mill, and across the dirt-floored courtyard to the dormitory. It was almost suppertime, and when the children walked inside they could see the other employees sitting on their bunks and talking quietly among themselves.

"I see you're back," one of the workers said. "I'm surprised you can show your faces around here, after what you did to Phil."

"Oh, come now," Phil said, and the orphans turned to see him lying down on his bunk with his leg in a cast. "Klaus didn't mean to do it, did you, Klaus?"

"Mean to do what?" Klaus asked quizzically, a word which here means "because he didn't know that he caused the accident that hurt Phil's leg."

"Our brother is very tired," Violet said quickly. "How are you feeling, Phil?"

"Oh, perfectly fine," Phil said. "My leg hurts, but nothing else does. I'm really quite fortunate. But enough about me. There's a memo that was left for you. Foreman Flacutono said it was very important."

Phil handed Violet an envelope with the word "Baudelaires" typed on the front, just like the typed note of welcome the children had found on their first day at the mill. Inside the envelope was a note, which read as follows:

Memorandum

To: The Baudelaire Orphans

From: \Sir

Subject: Today's Accident

I have been informed that you caused an accident this morning at the mill that injured an employee and disrupted the day's work.

Accidents are caused by bad workers, and bad workers are not tolerated at the Lucky Smells Lumbermill. If you continue to cause accidents I will be forced to fire you and send you to live elsewhere. I have located a nice young lady who lives in town who would be happy to adopt three young children. Her name is Shirley and she works as a receptionist. If the three of you continue to be bad workers, I will place you under her care.

CHAPTER
Ten

Violet read the memo out loud to her siblings, and she didn't know whose reaction was more upsetting. As Sunny heard the bad news, she bit her lip in worry. Her tooth was so sharp that tiny drops of blood dribbled down her chin, and this was certainly upsetting. But Klaus didn't seem to hear the memo at all. He just stared into space, and this was worrisome as well. Violet put the memo back into the envelope, sat on the bottom bunk, and wondered what in the world she could do.

"Bad news?" Phil said sympathetically.

"Remember, sometimes something might seem like bad news, but it could turn out to be a blessing in disguise."

Violet tried to smile at Phil, but her smiling muscles just stayed put. She knew—or she thought she knew, anyway, because she was actually wrong—that the only thing in disguise was Count Olaf. "We have to go see Sir," Violet said finally. "We have to explain to him what has happened."

"You're not supposed to see Sir without an appointment," Phil said.

"This is an emergency," Violet said. "Come on, Sunny. Come on . . ." She looked at her brother, who looked back at his older sister with wide, wide eyes. Violet remembered the accident he had caused, and all the previous Baudelaire guardians who had been destroyed. She could not imagine that Klaus would be capable of the sort of heinous murders that Count Olaf had committed, but she could not be sure. Not when he was hypnotized.

"Dinel," Sunny said.

"Klaus simply cannot go," Violet decided. "Phil, will you please keep an eye on our brother while we go and visit Sir?"

"Of course," Phil said.

"A *very close eye*," she emphasized, leading Klaus to the Baudelaire bunk. "He's . . . he's not been himself lately, as I'm sure you've noticed. Please make sure he stays out of trouble."

"I will," Phil promised.

"Now, Klaus," Violet said, "please get some sleep, and I hope you'll feel better in the morning."

"Wub," Sunny said, which meant something along the lines of "I hope so, too."

Klaus lay down on the bunk, and his sisters looked at his bare feet, which were filthy from walking around all day without any shoes on. "Good night, Violet," Klaus said. "Good night, Susan."

"Her name is *Sunny*," Violet said.

"I'm sorry," Klaus said. "I'm just so exhausted.

Do you really think I will feel better in the morning?"

"If we're lucky," Violet said. "Now, go to sleep."

Klaus glanced at his older sister. "Yes, sir," he said, quietly. He shut his eyes and immediately fell asleep. The eldest Baudelaire tucked the blanket around her brother and took a long, worried glance at him. Then she took Sunny's hand and, with a smile to Phil, walked back out of the dormitory and across the courtyard to the offices. Inside, the two Baudelaires walked past the mirror without even a glance at their reflections, and knocked on the door.

"Come in!" The children recognized the booming voice of Sir, and nervously opened the door to the office. Sir was sitting at an enormous desk made of dark, dark wood, still smoking a cigar so his face could not be seen behind the cloud of smoke. The desk was covered with papers and folders, and there was a nameplate that read "The Boss" in letters made of chewed-up gum, just like the lumbermill sign outside. It was difficult to see the rest of the room, because there was only one tiny light in the room, which sat on Sir's desk. Next to Sir stood Charles, who gave the children a shy smile as they walked up to their guardian.

"Do you have an appointment?" Sir asked.

"No," Violet said, "but it's very important that I talk to you."

"I'll decide what's very important!" Sir barked. "You see this nameplate? It says 'The Boss,' and that's who I am! It's very important when *I* say it's very important, understand?"

"Yes, Sir," Violet said, "but I think you'll agree with me when I explain what's been going on."

"I *know* what's been going on," Sir said. "I'm the boss! Of course I know! Didn't you get my memo about the accident?"

Violet took a deep breath and looked Sir in the eye, or at least the part of the cloud of smoke where she thought his eye probably was. "The accident," she said finally, "happened because Klaus was hypnotized."

"What your brother does for a hobby is none of my concern," Sir said, "and it doesn't excuse accidents."

"You don't understand, Sir," Violet said. "Klaus was hypnotized by Dr. Orwell, who is in cahoots with Count Olaf."

"Oh no!" Charles said. "You poor children! Sir, we have to put a stop to this!"

"We *are* putting a stop to this!" Sir said. "You children will cause no more accidents, and you'll be safely employed by this lumbermill. Otherwise, out you go!"

"Sir!" Charles cried. "You wouldn't throw the children out into the street!"

"Of course not," Sir said. "As I explained in my memo, I met a very nice young lady who works as a receptionist. When I mentioned there were three children in my care, she said that if you were ever any trouble, she'd take you, because she'd always wanted children of her own."

"Palsh!" Sunny cried.

"That's Count Olaf!" Violet cried.

"Do I look like an idiot to you?" Sir asked, pointing to his cloud. "I have a complete description of Count Olaf from Mr. Poe, and this receptionist looked nothing like him. She was a very nice lady."

"Did you look for the tattoo?" Charles asked. "Count Olaf has a tattoo on his ankle, remember?"

"Of course I didn't look for the tattoo," Sir said impatiently. "It's not polite to look at a woman's legs."

"But she's not a woman!" Violet burst out. "I mean, *he's* not a woman! He's Count Olaf!"

"I saw her nameplate," Sir said. "It didn't say 'Count Olaf.' It said 'Shirley.'"

"Fiti!" Sunny shrieked, which you already know meant "That nameplate doesn't prove anything, of course!" But Violet did not have time to translate, because Sir was pounding his hands on the desk.

"Hypnosis! Count Olaf! Fiti! I've had enough of your excuses!" he yelled. "Your job is to work hard at the lumbermill, not cause accidents! I am busy enough without having to deal with clumsy children!"

Quickly, Violet thought of something else. "Well, can we call Mr. Poe?" she asked. "He knows all about Count Olaf, so perhaps he can be helpful." Violet did not add that Mr. Poe was not usually a very helpful person.

"You want to add the cost of a long-distance phone call to the burden of caring for you?" Sir asked. "I think not. Let me put it to you in the simplest way I can: If you screw up again, I will give you away to Shirley."

"Now, Sir," Charles said. "These are children. You shouldn't talk to them this way. As you remember, I never thought it was a good idea for the Baudelaires to work in the mill.

They should be treated like members of the family."

"They *are* being treated like members of the family," Sir said. "Many of my cousins live there in the dormitory. I refuse to argue with you, Charles! You're my partner! Your job is to iron my shirts and cook my omelettes, not boss me around!"

"You're right, of course," Charles said softly. "I'm sorry."

"Now get out of here, all of you!" Sir barked. "I have lots of work to do!"

Sunny opened her mouth to say something, but she knew it would be useless. Violet thought of something else she could point out, but she knew it would be worthless. And Charles started to raise his hand to make a point, but he knew it would be bootless, a word which here means "useless and worthless." So Charles and the two Baudelaires left the dark office without another word, and stood for a moment together in the hallway.

"Don't worry," Charles whispered. "I'll help you."

"How?" Violet whispered back. "Will you call Mr. Poe and tell him Count Olaf is here?"

"Ulo?" Sunny asked, which meant "Will you have Dr. Orwell arrested?"

"Will you hide us from Shirley?" Violet asked.

"Henipul?" Sunny asked, which meant "Will you undo Klaus's hypnotism?"

"No," Charles admitted. "I can't do any of those things. Sir would get mad at me, and we can't have that. But tomorrow, I will try and sneak you some raisins at lunchtime. O.K.?"

It was not O.K., of course, not at all. Raisins are healthy, and they are inexpensive, and some people may even find them delicious. But they are rarely considered helpful. In fact, raisins were one of the least helpful things Charles could offer, if he really wanted to help. But Violet didn't answer him. She was looking down the hallway and thinking. Sunny didn't answer him either, because she was already crawling toward the door to the library. The Baudelaire sisters had no time to talk with Charles. They had to figure out a plan, and they had to figure it out quickly. The Baudelaire orphans were in a very difficult situation, and they needed every available moment to come up with something much, much more helpful than raisins.

Eleven

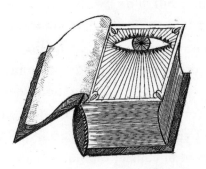

As we have discussed previously, a book's first sentence can often tell you what sort of story the book contains. This book, you will remember, began with the sentence "The Baudelaire orphans looked out the grimy window of the train and gazed at the gloomy blackness of the Finite Forest, wondering if their lives would ever get any better," and the story has certainly been as wretched and hopeless as the first sentence promised it would be. I only bring this up now so you can understand the feeling of dread that Violet and Sunny Baudelaire experienced as they opened a book in the library of the Lucky Smells Lumbermill. The two Baudelaire sisters already had a feeling of dread, of course. Part of the dread came from how cruelly unfairly Sir had behaved. Another part of the dread came from how Charles, kind as he was, seemed unable to help them. Yet another part of the dread came from the fact that Klaus had been hypnotized once more. And of course, the lion's share of the dread—the phrase "lion's share" here means "the biggest part" and has nothing to do with lions or sharing—came from the fact that Count Olaf—or, as he insisted on calling himself, Shirley—was back in the Baudelaires' lives and causing so much misery.

But there was an extra helping of dread that Violet and Sunny felt when they began *Advanced Ocular Science*, by Dr. Georgina Orwell. The first sentence was "This tome will endeavor to scrutinize, in quasi-inclusive breadth, the epistemology of ophthalmologically contrived appraisals of ocular systems and the subsequent and requisite exertions imperative for expungation of injurious states," and as Violet read it out loud to her sister, both children felt the dread that comes when you begin a very boring and difficult book.

"Oh dear," Violet said, wondering what in the world "tome" meant. "This is a very difficult book."

"Garj!" Sunny said, wondering what in the world "endeavor" meant.

"If only we had a dictionary," Violet said glumly. "Then we might be able to figure out what this sentence means."

"Yash!" Sunny pointed out, which meant something like "And if only Klaus weren't hypnotized, then he could *tell* us what this sentence means."

Violet and Sunny sighed, and thought of their poor hypnotized brother. Klaus seemed so different from the brother they knew that it was almost as if Count Olaf had already succeeded with his dastardly scheme, and destroyed one of the Baudelaire orphans. Klaus usually looked interested in the world around him, and now he had a blank expression on his face. His eyes were usually all squinty from reading, and now they were wide as if he had been watching TV instead. He was usually alert, and full of interesting things to say, and now he was forgetful, and almost completely silent.

"Who knows if Klaus could define these words for us?" Violet asked. "He said it felt like part of his brain had been wiped clean. Maybe he doesn't know all those words when he's hypnotized. I don't think I've heard him define anything since the accident with Phil, when he explained the word 'inordinate.' You might as well get some rest, Sunny. I'll wake you up if I read anything useful."

Sunny crawled up on the table and lay down next to *Advanced Ocular Science*, which was almost as big as she was. Violet gazed at her sister for

a moment, and then turned her attention to
the book. Violet liked to read, of course, but at
heart she was an inventor, not a researcher. She
simply did not have Klaus's amazing reading
skills. Violet stared at Dr. Orwell's first sentence
again, and just saw a mess of difficult words.
She knew that if Klaus were in the library, and
not hypnotized, he would see a way to help
them out of their situation. Violet began to
imagine how her brother would go about reading *Advanced Ocular Science*, and tried to copy his
methods.

First she turned back the pages of the book,
back before even the first page, to the table of
contents, which as I'm sure you know is a list of
the titles and page numbers of each chapter in
a book. Violet had paid scarcely any attention to
it when she first opened the book, but she realized that Klaus would probably examine the
table of contents first, so he could see which
chapters of the book might be most helpful.
Quickly she scanned the table of contents:

1. Introduction   1

2. Basic Ophthalmology   105

3. Nearsightedness and Farsightedness   279

4. Blindness   311

5. Itchy Eyelashes   398

6. Damaged Pupils   501

7. Blinking Problems   612

8. Winking Problems   650

9. Surgical Practices   783

10. Glasses, Monocles, and Contact Lenses   857

11. Sunglasses   926

12. Hypnosis and Mind Control   927

13. Which Eye Color Is the Best One?   1,000

Immediately, of course, Violet saw that chapter twelve would be the most helpful, and was glad she'd thought of looking at the table of contents instead of reading 927 pages until she found something helpful. Grateful that she could skip that daunting first paragraph—the word "daunting" here means "full of incredibly difficult words"—she flipped through *Advanced*

Ocular Science until she reached "Hypnosis and Mind Control."

The phrase "stylistic consistency" is used to describe books that are similar from start to finish. For instance, the book you are reading right now has stylistic consistency, because it began in a miserable way and will continue that way until the last page. I'm sorry to say that Violet realized, as she began chapter twelve, that Dr. Orwell's book had stylistic consistency as well. The first sentence of "Hypnosis and Mind Control" was "Hypnosis is an efficacious yet precarious methodology and should not be assayed by neophytes," and it was every bit as difficult and boring as the first sentence of the whole book. Violet reread the sentence, and then reread it again, and her heart began to sink. How in the world did Klaus do it? When the three children lived in the Baudelaire home, there was a huge dictionary in their parents' library, and Klaus would often use it to help him with difficult books. But how did Klaus read difficult books when there was no dictionary to be found? It was a puzzle, and Violet knew it was a puzzle she had to solve quickly.

She turned her attention back to the book, and reread the sentence one more time, but this time she simply skipped the words she did not know. As often happens when one reads in this way, Violet's brain made a little humming noise as she encountered each word—or each part of a word—she did not know. So inside her head, the opening sentence of chapter twelve read as follows: "'Hypnosis is an *hmmm* yet *hmmm* method *hmmm* and should not be *hmmm*ed by *hmmm*s,'" and although she could not tell exactly what it meant, she could guess. "It could mean," she guessed to herself, "that hypnosis is a difficult method and should not be learned by amateurs," and the interesting thing is that she was not too far off. The night grew later and later, and Violet continued to read the chapter in this way, and she was surprised to learn that she could guess her way through pages and pages of

Dr. Orwell's book. This is not the best way to read, of course, because you can make horribly wrong guesses, but it will do in an emergency.

For several hours, the Lucky Smells library was completely quiet except for the turning of pages, as Violet read the book searching for anything helpful. Every so often she glanced at her sister, and for the first time in her life Violet wished that Sunny were older than she was. When you are trying to figure out a difficult problem—such as the problem of trying to get your brother unhypnotized so as not to be placed into the hands of a greedy man disguised as a receptionist—it is often helpful to discuss the problem with other people in order to come up with a quick and useful solution. Violet remembered that, when the Baudelaires were living with Aunt Josephine, it had been extremely helpful to talk to Klaus about a note that turned out to have a secret hidden within it. But with Sunny it was different. The youngest Baudelaire was charming, and well toothed, and quite intelligent for a baby. But she was still a baby, and as Violet *hmm*ed through chapter twelve, she worried that she would fail to find a solution with only a baby as a discussion partner. Nevertheless, when she found a sentence that appeared to be useful, she gave Sunny a waking nudge and read the sentence out loud.

"Listen to this, Sunny," she said, when her sister opened her eyes. "'Once a subject has been hypnotized, a simple *hmmm* word will make him or her perform whatever *hmmm* acts any *hmmm* wants *hmmm*ed.'"

"*Hmmm?*" Sunny asked.

"Those are the words I don't know," Violet explained. "It's difficult to read this way, but I can guess what Dr. Orwell means. I think she means that once you've hypnotized someone, all you need to do is say a certain word and they will obey you. Remember what Klaus told us he learned from the *Encyclopedia Hypnotica*? There was that Egyptian king who did chicken imitations, and the merchant who played the violin, and that writer, and all the hypnotists did was say a certain word. But they were all different words. I wonder which word applies to Klaus."

"Heece," Sunny said, which probably meant something like "Beats me. I'm only a baby."

Violet gave her a gentle smile and tried to imagine what Klaus would have said if he had been there, unhypnotized, in the library with his sisters. "I'll search for more information," she decided.

"Brewol," Sunny said, which meant "And I'll go back to sleep."

Both Baudelaires were true to their word, and for a time the library was silent again. Violet *hmmm*ed through the book and grew more and more exhausted and worried. There were only a few hours left until the working day began, and she was scared that her efforts would be as ineffectual—the word "ineffectual" here means "unable to get Klaus unhypnotized"—as if she had low self-esteem. But just as she was about to fall asleep beside her sister, she found a passage in the book that seemed so useful she read it out loud immediately, waking Sunny up in the process.

"'In order to *hmmm* the hypnotic hold on the *hmmm*,'" Violet said, "'the same method *hmmm* is used: a *hmmm* word, uttered out loud, will *hmmm* the *hmmm* immediately.' I think Dr. Orwell is talking about getting people un-hypnotized, and it has to do with another word being uttered out loud. If we figure *that* one out, we can unhypnotize Klaus, and we won't fall into Shirley's clutches."

"Skel," Sunny said, rubbing her eyes. She probably meant something like "But I wonder what that word could be."

"I don't know," Violet said, "but we'd better figure it out before it's too late."

"Hmmm," Sunny said, making a humming noise because she was thinking, rather than because she was reading a word she did not know.

"Hmmm," Violet said, which meant *she* was thinking, too. But then there was another *hmmm* that made the two Baudelaire sisters look at one another in worry. This was not the *hmmm* of a brain that did not know what a word meant, or the *hmmm* of a person thinking. This *hmmm* was much longer and louder, and it was a *hmmm* that made the Baudelaire sisters stop their thinking and hurry out of the library, clutching Dr. Orwell's book in their trembling hands. It was the *hmmm* of the lumbermill's saw. Somebody had turned on the mill's deadliest machine in the early, early hours of morning.

Violet and Sunny hurried across the courtyard, which was quite dark in the first few rays of the sun. Hurriedly they opened the doors of the mill and looked inside. Foreman Flacutono was standing near the entrance, with his back to the two girls, pointing a finger and giving an order. The rusty sawing machine was whirring away, making that dreadful humming sound, and there was a log on the ground, all ready to be pushed into the saw. The log seemed to be covered in layers and layers of string—the string that had been inside the string machine, before Klaus had smashed it.

The two sisters took a better look, stepping farther into the mill, and saw that the string was wrapped around something else, tying a large bundle to the log. And when they took an even better look, peeking from behind Foreman Flacutono, they saw that the bundle was Charles. He was tied to the log with so much string that he looked a bit like a cocoon, except that a cocoon had never looked this frightened. Layers of string were covering his mouth, so he could not make a sound, but his eyes were uncovered and he was staring in terror at the saw as it drew closer and closer.

"Yes, you little twerp," Foreman Flacutono was saying. "You've been fortunate so far, avoiding my boss's clutches, but no more. One more accident and you'll be ours, and this will be the worst accident the lumbermill has ever seen. Just imagine Sir's displeasure when he learns that his partner has been sliced into human boards. Now, you lucky man, go and push the log into the saw!"

Violet and Sunny took a few more steps forward, near enough that they could reach out and touch Foreman Flacutono—not that they wanted to do such a disgusting thing, of course—and saw their brother. Klaus was standing at the controls of the sawing machine in his bare feet, staring at the foreman with his wide, blank eyes.

"Yes, sir," he said, and Charles's eyes grew wide with panic.

"Klaus!" Violet cried. "Klaus, don't do it!"

Foreman Flacutono whirled around, his beady eyes glaring from over his surgical mask. "Why, if it isn't the other two midgets," he said. "You're just in time to see the accident."

"It's not an accident," Violet said. "You're doing it on purpose!"

"Let's not split hairs," the foreman said, using an expression which here means "argue over something that's not at all important."

"You've been in on this all the time!" Violet shouted. "You're in cahoots with Dr. Orwell, and Shirley!"

"So what?" Foreman Flacutono said.

"Deluny!" Sunny shrieked, which meant something along the lines of "You're not just a bad foreman—you're an evil person!"

"I don't know what you mean, little midget," Foreman Flacutono said, "and I don't care. Klaus, you lucky boy, please continue."

"No, Klaus!" Violet shouted. "No!"

"Kewtu!" Sunny shrieked.

"Your words will do no good," Foreman Flacutono said. "See?"

Sunny saw, all right, as she watched her barefoot brother walking over to the log as if his sisters had not spoken. But Violet was not looking at her brother. She was looking at Foreman Flacutono, and thinking of everything he had said. The terrible foreman was right, of course. The words of the two unhypnotized Baudelaires would do no good. But Violet knew that some words would help. The book she was holding had told her, in between *hmmm*s, that there was a word that was used to command Klaus, and a word that would unhypnotize him. The eldest Baudelaire realized that Foreman Flacutono must have used the command word just now, and she was trying to remember everything that he had said. He'd called Klaus a twerp, but it seemed unlikely that "twerp" would be the word. He'd said "log" and he'd said "push," but those didn't seem likely either. She realized with despair that the command word could almost be anything.

"That's right," Foreman Flacutono said, as Klaus reached the log. "Now, in the name of Lucky Smells Lumbermill, push the log in the path of the saw."

Violet closed her eyes and racked her brain, a phrase which here means "tried to think of other times the command word must have been used." Foreman Flacutono must have used it when Klaus caused the first accident, the one that broke Phil's leg. "*You*, you lucky midget," Violet remembered the foreman had said, "will be operating the machine," and Klaus had said "Yes, sir" in that faint, hypnotized voice, the same voice he had used before he had gone to sleep just the previous night.

"Egu!" Sunny shrieked in fear, as the *hmmm* of the saw grew louder and rougher. Klaus had pushed the log up to the saw, and Charles's eyes grew even wider as the blade began to slice the wood, getting closer and closer to where Charles was tied up.

As she remembered Klaus's "Yes, sir," before he went to sleep, Violet realized she must have used the command word herself, by accident. She racked her brain again, straining to remember the conversation. Klaus had called his baby sister Susan, instead of Sunny, and then asked if he would really feel better in the morning. But what had Violet replied?

"Keep pushing, you lucky midget," Foreman Flacutono said, and Violet knew in an instant.

Lucky.

"*Lucky!*" the eldest Baudelaire shouted, not bothering to hide the word in a sentence, as the foreman did. "Push the log away from the saw, Klaus!"

"Yes, sir," Klaus said quietly, and the Baude- laire sisters saw with relief that he pushed the log away from the whirling blade just as Charles's toes were about to be sliced. Foreman Flacutono whirled around and stared at Violet in beady rage. She knew that he knew that she knew.

"*Lucky!*" he snarled. "Push the log back toward the saw, Klaus!"

"Yes, sir," Klaus muttered.

"*Lucky!*" Violet cried. "Push the log away!"

"Yes, sir," Klaus murmured.

"*Lucky!*" Foreman Flacutono barked. "Toward the saw!"

"Lucky away!"

"Lucky toward the saw!"

"Lucky away!"

"Lucky toward the saw!"

"LUCKY!" bellowed a new voice from the doorway, and everyone—including Violet, Klaus, Sunny, and Foreman Flacutono—turned around. Even Charles tried the best he could to see Dr. Orwell, who had appeared in the doorway along with Shirley, who was lurking behind the hypnotist.

"We just stopped by to make sure everything went well," Dr. Orwell said, gesturing to the saw with her black cane. "And I'm certainly glad we did. *Lucky!*" she shouted to Klaus. "Do not listen to your sisters!"

"What a good idea," Foreman Flacutono said the doctor. "I never thought of that."

"That's why you're only a foreman," Dr. Orwell replied snobbily. "*Lucky*, Klaus! Push the log in the path of the saw!"

"Yes, sir," Klaus said, and began to push the log again.

"*Please*, Klaus!" Violet cried. "Don't do this!"

"Gice!" Sunny shrieked, which meant "Don't hurt Charles!"

"*Please*, Dr. Orwell!" Violet cried. "Don't force my brother to do this terrible thing!"

"It *is* a terrible thing, I know," Dr. Orwell said. "But it's a terrible thing that the Baudelaire fortune goes to you three brats, instead of to me and Shirley. We're going to split the money fifty-fifty."

"After expenses, Georgina," Shirley reminded her.

"After expenses, of course," Dr. Orwell said. The *hmmm* of the saw began making its louder, rougher sound as the blade started to slice the log once more. Tears appeared in Charles's eyes and began to run down the string tying him to the log. Violet looked at her brother, and then at Dr. Orwell, and dropped the heavy book on the ground in frustration. What she needed now, and most desperately, was the word that would unhypnotize her brother, but she had no idea what it could be. The command word had been used many times, and Violet had been able to figure out which word had been used over and over. But Klaus had only been unhypnotized once, after the accident that had broken Phil's leg. She and her sister had known, in the moment he started defining a word for the employees, that Klaus was back to normal, but who knew what word caused him, that afternoon, to suddenly stop following Foreman Flacutono's orders? Violet looked from Charles's tears to the ones appearing in Sunny's eyes as the fatal accident grew nearer and nearer. In a moment, it seemed, they would watch Charles die a horrible death, and then they would most certainly be placed in Shirley's care. After so many narrow escapes from Count Olaf's treachery, this seemed to be the moment of his—or in this case, *her*—

terrible triumph. Out of all the situations, Violet thought to herself, that she and her siblings had been in, this was the most miserably irregular. It was the most miserably immoderate. It was the most miserably disorderly. It was the most miserably excessive. And as she thought all these words she thought of the one that had unhypnotized Klaus, the one that just might save all their lives.

"Inordinate!" she shouted, as loudly as she could to be heard over the terrible noise of the saw. *"Inordinate! Inordinate! Inordinate!"*

Klaus blinked, and then looked all around him as if somebody had just dropped him in the middle of the mill. "Where am I?" he asked.

"Oh, Klaus," Violet said in relief. "You're here with us!"

"Drat!" Dr. Orwell said. "He's unhypnotized! How in the world would a child know a complicated word like 'inordinate'?"

"These brats know lots of words," Shirley said, in her ridiculously fake high voice.

"They're book addicts. But we can still create an accident and win the fortune!"

"Oh no you can't!" Klaus cried, and stepped forward to push Charles out of the way.

"Oh yes we can!" Foreman Flacutono said, and stuck his foot out again. You would think that such a trick would only work a maximum of two times, but in this case you would be wrong, and in this case Klaus fell to the floor again, his head clanging against the pile of debarkers and tiny green boxes.

"Oh no you can't!" Violet cried, and stepped forward to push Charles out of the way herself.

"Oh yes we can!" Shirley said, in her silly high voice, and grabbed Violet's arm. Foreman Flacutono quickly grabbed her other arm, and the eldest Baudelaire found herself trapped.

"Oh toonoy!" Sunny cried, and crawled toward Charles. She was not strong enough to push the log away from the saw, but she thought she could bite through his string and set him free.

"Oh yes we can!" Dr. Orwell said, and

reached down to grab the youngest Baudelaire. But Sunny was ready. Quckly she opened her mouth and bit down on the hypnotist's hand as hard as she could.

"*Gack!*" Dr. Orwell shouted, using an expression that is in no particular language. But then she smiled and used an expression that was in French: "*En garde!*" "En garde!," as you may know, is an expression people use when they wish to announce the beginning of a sword-fight, and with a wicked smile, Dr. Orwell pressed the red jewel on top of her black cane, and a shiny blade emerged from the opposite end. In just one second, her cane had become a sword, which she then pointed at the youngest Baudelaire orphan. But Sunny, being only an infant, had no sword. She only had her four sharp teeth, and, looking Dr. Orwell right in the eye, she opened her mouth and pointed all four at this despicable person.

There is a loud *clink!* noise that a sword makes when it hits another sword—or, in this case, a tooth—and whenever I hear it I am reminded of a swordfight I was forced to have with a television repairman not long ago. Sunny, however, was only reminded of how much she did not want to be sliced to bits. Dr. Orwell swung her cane-sword at Sunny, and Sunny swung her teeth at Dr. Orwell, and soon the *clink!* noises were almost as loud as the sawing machine which continued to saw up the log toward Charles. *Clink!* Up, up, the blade inched until it was only a hair's breadth—the expression "hair's breadth" here means "a teeny-tiny measurement"—away from Charles's foot.

"Klaus!" Violet cried, struggling in the grips of Shirley and Foreman Flacutono. "Do something!"

"Your brother can't do anything!" Shirley said, giggling in a most annoying way. "He's just been unhypnotized—he's too dazed to do anything. Foreman Flacutono, let's both pull! We can make Violet's armpits sore that way!"

Shirley was right about Violet's sore armpits,

but she was wrong about Klaus. He *had* just
been unhypnotized, and he *was* quite dazed,
but he wasn't too dazed to do anything. The
trouble was, he simply couldn't think of what to
do. Klaus had been thrown into the corner with
the debarkers and the gum, and if he moved in
the direction of Charles, or Violet, he would
walk right into Sunny and Dr. Orwell's swordfight, and as he heard another *clink!* from the
sword hitting Sunny's tooth he knew he would
be seriously wounded if he tried to walk through
the dueling pair. But over the *clink!*s he heard
an even louder and even rougher noise from the
sawing machine, and Klaus saw with horror that
the blade was beginning to slice through the
soles of Charles's shoes. Sir's partner tried
to wiggle his feet away from the blade, but
they were tied too tightly, and tiny shoe-sole
shavings began to fall to the floor of the mill. In
a moment the blade would be finished with the
sole of Charles's shoe and begin on the sole of
Charles's foot. Klaus needed to invent something

to stop the machine, and he needed to invent it right away.

Klaus stared at the circular blade of the saw, and his heart began to sink. How in the world did Violet do it? Klaus had a mild interest in mechanical things, but at heart he was a reader, not an inventor. He simply did not have Violet's amazing inventing skills. He looked at the machine and just saw a deadly device, but he knew that if Violet were in this corner of the mill, and not getting sore armpits from Shirley and Foreman Flacutono, she would see a way to help them out of their situation. Klaus tried to imagine how his sister would go about inventing something right there on the spot, and tried to copy her methods.

Clink! Klaus looked around him for inventing materials, but saw only debarkers and tiny green boxes of gum. Immediately he ripped open a box of gum and shoved several pieces into his mouth, chewing ferociously. The expression "gum up the works" does not actually have to do with gum, but merely refers to something that stops the progress of something else. Klaus chewed and chewed the gum, hoping that the stickiness of the gum could gum up the works of the sawing machine, and stop the deadly progress of its blade.

Clink! Sunny's third tooth hit the blade of Dr. Orwell's sword, and Klaus quickly spat the gum out of his mouth into his hand and threw it at the machine as hard as he could. But it merely fell to the ground with a wet *plop!* Klaus realized that gum didn't weigh enough to reach the machine. Like a feather, or a piece of paper, the wad of gum simply couldn't be thrown very far.

Hukkita—hukkita—hukkita! The machine began making the loudest and roughest sound Klaus had ever heard. Charles closed his eyes, and Klaus knew that the blade must have hit the bottom of his foot. He grabbed a bigger handful of gum and shoved it into his mouth, but he didn't know if he could chew enough gum to make a heavy enough invention. Unable to watch the saw any longer, he looked down, and when his eye fell upon one of the debarkers he knew he could invent something after all.

When Klaus looked at the lumbermill equipment, he remembered a time when he was even more bored than he had been when working at Lucky Smells. This especially boring time had happened a very long time ago, when the Baudelaire parents were still alive. Klaus had read a book on different kinds of fish, and asked his parents if they would take him fishing. His mother warned him that fishing was one of the most boring activities in the world, but found two fishing poles in the basement and agreed to take him to a nearby lake. Klaus had been hoping that he would get to see the different types of fish he had read about, but instead he and his mother sat in a rowboat in the middle of a lake and did nothing for an entire afternoon. He and his mother had to keep quiet, so as not to scare the fish away, but there were no fish, no conversation, and absolutely no fun. You might think that Klaus would not want to remember such a boring time, particularly in the middle of a crisis, but one detail of this very boring afternoon turned out to be extremely helpful.

As Sunny struggled with Dr. Orwell, Violet struggled with Shirley and Foreman Flacutono, and poor Charles struggled with the saw, Klaus remembered the part of the fishing process known as casting. Casting is the process of using one's fishing pole to throw one's fishing line out into the middle of the lake in order to try to catch a fish. In the case of Klaus and his mother, the casting hadn't worked, but Klaus did not want to catch fish. He wanted to save Charles's life.

Quickly, the middle Baudelaire grabbed the debarker and spat his gum onto one end of it. He was planning to use the sticky gum as a sort of fishing line and the debarker as a sort of fishing pole, in order to throw gum all the way to the saw. Klaus's invention looked more like a wad of gum at the end of a strip of metal than a real fishing pole, but Klaus didn't care how it looked. He only cared whether it could stop the saw. He took a deep breath, and cast the debarker the way his mother taught him to cast his fishing pole.

Plop! To Klaus's delight, the gum stretched over Dr. Orwell and Sunny, who were still fighting, just as fishing line will stretch out across the surface of a lake. But to Klaus's horror, the gum did not land on the saw. It landed on the string that was tying the wriggling Charles to the log. Klaus watched Charles wriggle and was once again reminded of a fish, and it occurred to him that perhaps his invention had worked after all. Gathering up all of his strength—and, after working at a lumbermill for a while, he actually had quite a bit of strength for a young boy—he grabbed his invention, and pulled. Klaus pulled on his debarker, and the debarker pulled on the gum, and the gum pulled on the log, and to the relief of all three Baudelaire orphans the log moved to one side. It did not move very far, and it did not move very quickly, and it certainly did not move very gracefully, but it moved enough. The horrible noise stopped, and the blade of the saw kept slicing, but the log was far enough out of the way that the machine was simply slicing thin air. Charles looked at Klaus, and his eyes filled with tears, and when Sunny turned to look she saw that Klaus was crying, too.

But when Sunny turned to look, Dr. Orwell saw her chance. With a swing of one of her big ugly boots, she kicked Sunny to the ground and held her in place with one foot. Then, standing over the infant, she raised her sword high in the air and began to laugh a loud, horrible snarl of a laugh. "I do believe," she said, cackling, "that there will be an accident at Lucky Smells Lumbermill after all!"

And Dr. Orwell was right. There *was* an accident at the lumbermill, after all, a fatal accident, which is a phrase used to describe one that kills somebody. For just as Dr. Orwell was about to bring her sword down on little Sunny's throat, the door of the lumbermill opened and Sir walked into the room. "What in the world is going on?" he barked, and Dr. Orwell turned to him, absolutely surprised. When people are absolutely surprised, they sometimes take a step backward, and taking a step backward can sometimes lead to an accident. Such was the case at this moment, for when Dr. Orwell stepped backward, she stepped into the path of the whirring saw, and there was a very ghastly accident indeed.

CHAPTER
Thirteen

"*Dreadful*, dreadful, dreadful," Sir said, shaking the cloud of smoke that covered his head. "Dreadful, dreadful, dreadful."

"I quite agree," Mr. Poe said, coughing into his handkerchief. "When you called me this morning and described the situation, I thought it was so dreadful that I canceled several important appointments and took the first available train to Paltryville, in order to handle this matter personally."

"We appreciate it very much," Charles said.

"Dreadful, dreadful, dreadful," Sir said again.

The Baudelaire orphans sat together on the floor of Sir's office and looked up at the adults discussing the situation, wondering how in the world they could talk about it so calmly. The word "dreadful," even when used three times in a row, did not seem like a dreadful enough word to describe everything that had happened. Violet was still trembling from how Klaus had looked while hypnotized. Klaus was still shivering from how Charles had almost been sliced up. Sunny was still shaking from how she had almost been killed in the swordfight with Dr. Orwell. And, of course, all three orphans were still shuddering from how Dr. Orwell had met her demise, a phrase which here means "stepped into the path of the sawing machine." The children felt as if they could barely speak at all, let alone participate in a conversation.

"It's unbelievable," Sir said, "that Dr. Orwell was really a hypnotist, and that she hypnotized Klaus in order to get ahold of the Baudelaire fortune. Luckily, Violet figured out how to unhypnotize her brother, and he didn't cause any more accidents."

"It's unbelievable," Charles said, "that Foreman Flacutono grabbed me in the middle of the night, and tied me to that log, in order to get ahold of the Baudelaire fortune. Luckily, Klaus invented something that shoved the log out of the path of the saw just in time, and I only have a small cut on my foot."

"It's unbelievable," Mr. Poe said, after a short cough, "that Shirley was going to adopt the children, in order to get ahold of the Baudelaire fortune. Luckily, we realized her plan, and now she has to go back to being a receptionist."

At this Violet could keep quiet no longer. "Shirley is not a receptionist!" she cried. "She's not even Shirley! She's Count Olaf!"

"Now *that*," Sir said, "is the part of the story

that is so unbelievable that I don't believe it. I met this young woman, and she isn't at all like Count Olaf! She has one eyebrow instead of two, that's true, but plenty of wonderful people have that characteristic!"

"You must forgive the children," Mr. Poe said. "They tend to see Count Olaf everywhere."

"That's because he *is* everywhere," Klaus said bitterly.

"Well," Sir said, "he hasn't been here in Paltryville. We've been looking out for him, remember?"

"Weleef!" Sunny cried. She meant something along the lines of "But he was in disguise, as usual!"

"Can we go see this Shirley person?" Charles asked timidly. "The children do seem fairly sure of themselves. Perhaps if Mr. Poe could see this receptionist, we could clear this matter up."

"I put Shirley and Foreman Flacutono in the

library, and asked Phil to keep an eye on them," Sir said. "Charles's library turns out to be useful at last—as a substitute jail, until we clear up this matter!"

"The library was plenty useful, Sir," Violet said. "If I hadn't read up on hypnosis, your partner, Charles, would be dead."

"You certainly are a clever child," Charles said.

"Yes," Sir agreed. "You'll do wonderfully at boarding school."

"Boarding school?" Mr. Poe asked.

"Of course," Sir replied, nodding his cloud of smoke. "You don't think I would keep them now, do you, after all the trouble they've caused my lumbermill?"

"But that wasn't our fault!" Klaus cried.

"That doesn't matter," Sir said. "We made a deal. The deal was that I would try to keep Count Olaf away, and you wouldn't cause any more accidents. You didn't keep your end of the deal."

"Hech!" Sunny shrieked, which meant "But

you didn't keep your end of the deal, either!"
Sir paid no attention.

"Well, let's go see this woman," Mr. Poe
said, "and we can settle once and for all whether
or not Count Olaf was here."

The three grown-ups nodded, and the three
children followed them down the hallway to the
library door, where Phil was sitting on a chair
with a book in his hands.

"Hello, Phil," Violet said. "How is your leg?"

"Oh, it's getting better," he said, pointing to
his cast. "I've been guarding the door, Sir, and
neither Shirley nor Foreman Flacutono have
escaped. Oh, and by the way, I've been reading
this book, *The Paltryville Constitution*. I don't
understand all of the words, but it sounds like
it's illegal to pay people only in coupons."

"We'll talk about that later," Sir said quickly.
"We need to see Shirley about something."

Sir reached forward and opened the door to
reveal Shirley and Foreman Flacutono sitting
quietly at two tables near the window. Shirley

had Dr. Orwell's book in one hand and waved at the children with the other.

"Hello there, children!" she called, in her phony high voice. "I was so worried about you!"

"So was I!" Foreman Flacutono said. "Thank goodness I'm unhypnotized now, so I'm not treating you badly any longer!"

"So *you* were hypnotized, too?" Sir asked.

"Of course we were!" Shirley cried. She leaned down and patted all three children on the head. "We never would have acted so dreadfully otherwise, not to three such wonderful and delicate children!" Behind her false eyelashes, Shirley's shiny eyes gazed at the Baudelaires as if she were going to eat them as soon as she got the opportunity.

"You see?" Sir said to Mr. Poe. "No wonder it was unbelievable that Foreman Flacutono and Shirley acted so horribly. Of course she's not Count Olaf!"

"Count who?" Foreman Flacutono asked. "I've never heard of the man."

"Me neither," Shirley said, "but I'm only a receptionist."

"Perhaps you're not only a receptionist," Sir said. "Perhaps you're also a mother. What do you say, Mr. Poe? Shirley really wants to raise these children, and they're much too much trouble for me."

"No!" Klaus cried. "She's Count Olaf, not Shirley!"

Mr. Poe coughed into his white handkerchief at great length, and the three Baudelaires waited tensely for him to finish coughing and say something. Finally, he removed his handkerchief from his face and said to Shirley, "I'm sorry to say this, ma'am, but the children are convinced that you are a man named Count Olaf, disguised as a receptionist."

"If you'd like," Shirley said, "I can take you to Dr. Orwell's office—the *late* Dr. Orwell's office—and show you my nameplate. It clearly reads 'Shirley.'"

"I'm afraid that would not be sufficient," Mr. Poe said. "Would you do us all the courtesy of showing us your left ankle?"

"Why, it's not polite to look at a lady's legs," Shirley said. "Surely you know that."

"If your left ankle does not have a tattoo of an eye on it," Mr. Poe said, "then you are most certainly not Count Olaf."

Shirley's eyes shone very, very bright, and she gave everyone in the room a big, toothy smile. "And what if it *does*?" she asked, and hitched up her skirt slightly. "What if it *does* have a tattoo of an eye on it?"

Everyone's eyes turned to Shirley's ankle, and one eye looked back at them. It resembled the eye-shaped building of Dr. Orwell, which the Baudelaire orphans felt had been watching them since they arrived in Paltryville. It resembled the eye on the cover of Dr. Orwell's book, which the Baudelaire orphans felt had been staring at them since they began working at the Lucky Smells Lumbermill. And, of course, it looked exactly like Count Olaf's tattoo, which is what it was, and which the Baudelaire orphans felt had been gazing at them since their parents had died.

"In that case," Mr. Poe said, after a pause, "you are not Shirley. You are Count Olaf, and you are under arrest. I order you to take off that ridiculous disguise!"

"Should I take off my ridiculous disguise, as well?" Foreman Flacutono asked, and tore his white wig off with one smooth motion. It did not surprise the children that he was bald—they had known his absurd hair was a wig from the moment they laid eyes on him—but there was something about the shape of his bald head that suddenly seemed familiar. Glaring at the orphans with his beady eyes, he grabbed his surgical mask from his face and removed that, too. A long nose uncurled itself from where it had been pressed down to his face, and the siblings saw in an instant that it was one of Count

Olaf's assistants.

"It's the bald man!" Violet cried.

"With the long nose!" Klaus cried.

"Plemo!" Sunny cried, which meant "Who works for Count Olaf!"

"I guess we're lucky enough to capture *two* criminals today," Mr. Poe said sternly.

"Well, *three*, if you include Dr. Orwell," Count Olaf—and what a relief it is to call him that, instead of Shirley—said.

"Enough nonsense," Mr. Poe said. "You, Count Olaf, are under arrest for various murders and attempted murders, various frauds and attempted frauds, and various despicable acts and attempted despicable acts, and *you*, my bald, long-nosed friend, are under arrest for helping him."

Count Olaf shrugged, sending his wig toppling to the floor, and smiled at the Baudelaires in a way they were sorry to recognize. It was a certain smile that Count Olaf had just when it looked like he was trapped. It was a smile that looked as if Count Olaf were telling a joke, and it was a smile accompanied by his eyes shining brightly and his evil brain working furiously. "This book was certainly helpful to you, orphans," Count Olaf said, holding Dr. Orwell's *Advanced Ocular Science* high in the air, "and now it will help me." With all his rotten might, Count Olaf turned and threw the heavy book right through one of the library windows. With a crash of tinkling glass, the window shattered and left a good-sized hole. The hole was just big enough for a person to jump through, which is exactly what the bald man did, wrinkling his long nose at the children as if they smelled bad. Count Olaf laughed a horrible, rough laugh, and followed his comrade out the window and away from Paltryville. "I'll be back for you, orphans!" he called. "I'll be back for your lives!"

"Egad!" Mr. Poe said, using an expression which here means "Oh no! He's escaping!"

Sir stepped quickly to the window, and peered out after Count Olaf and the bald man, who were running as fast as their skinny legs could carry them. "Don't come back here!" Sir yelled out after them. "The orphans won't be here, so don't return!"

"What do you mean, the orphans won't be here?" Mr. Poe asked sternly. "You made a deal, and you didn't keep your end of it! Count Olaf was here after all!"

"That doesn't matter," Sir said, waving one of his hands dismissively. "Wherever these Baudelaires go, misfortune follows, and I will have no more of it!"

"But Sir," Charles said, "they're such good children!"

"I won't discuss it anymore," Sir said. "My nameplate says 'The Boss,' and that's who I am. The boss has the last word, and the last word is this: The children are no longer welcome at Lucky Smells!"

Violet, Klaus, and Sunny looked at one another. "The children are no longer welcome at Lucky Smells," of course, is not the last word, because it is many words, and they knew, of course, that when Sir said "the last word" he didn't mean one word, but the final opinion on the situation. But their experience at the lumbermill had been so very dreadful that they didn't care much that they were leaving Paltryville. Even a boarding school sounded like it would be better than their days with Foreman Flacutono, Dr. Orwell, and the evil Shirley. I'm sorry to tell you that the orphans were wrong about boarding school being better, but at the moment they knew nothing of the troubles ahead of them, only of the troubles behind them, and the troubles that had escaped out the window.

"Can we please discuss this matter later," Violet asked, "and call the police now? Maybe Count Olaf can be caught."

"Excellent idea, Violet," Mr. Poe said, although of course he should have thought of this idea earlier himself. "Sir, please take me to your telephone so we can call the authorities."

"Oh, all right," Sir said grumpily. "But remember, this is my last word on the matter. Charles, make me a milkshake. I'm very thirsty."

"Yes, Sir," Charles said, and limped after his partner and Mr. Poe, who were already out of the library. Halfway out the door, however, he stopped and smiled apologetically at the Baudelaires.

"I'm sorry," he said to them. "I'm sorry that I won't be seeing you anymore. But I guess Sir knows best."

"We're sorry too, Charles," Klaus said. "And I'm sorry that I caused you so much trouble."

"It wasn't your fault," Charles said kindly, as Phil limped up behind him.

"What happened?" Phil asked. "I heard breaking glass."

"Count Olaf got away," Violet said, and her heart sank as she realized it was really true. "Shirley was really Count Olaf in disguise, and he got away, just like he always does."

"Well, if you look on the bright side, you're really quite lucky," Phil said, and the orphans gave their optimistic friend a curious look and then looked curiously at one another. Once they had been happy children, so content and pleased with their life that they hadn't even known how happy they were. Then came the terrible fire, and it seemed since then that their lives had scarcely had one bright moment, let alone an entire bright side. From home to home they traveled, encountering misery and wretchedness wherever they went, and now the man who had caused such wretchedness had escaped once more. They certainly didn't feel very lucky.

"What do you mean?" Klaus asked quietly.

"Well, let me think," Phil said, and thought for a moment. In the background, the orphans could hear the dim sounds of Mr. Poe describing Count Olaf to somebody on the telephone. "You're alive," Phil said finally. "That's lucky. And I'm sure we can think of something else."

The three Baudelaire children looked at one another and then at Charles and Phil, the only people in Paltryville who had been kind to them. Although they would not miss the dormitory, or the terrible casseroles, or the back-breaking labor of the mill, the orphans would miss these two kind people. And as the siblings thought about whom they would miss, they thought how much they would have missed one another, if something even worse had happened to them. What if Sunny had lost the swordfight? What if Klaus had remained hypnotized for-ever? What if Violet had stepped into the path of the saw, instead of Dr. Orwell? The Baude-laires looked at the sunlight, pouring through the shattered window where Count Olaf had escaped, and shuddered to think of what could have happened. Being alive had never seemed lucky before, but as the children considered their terrible time in Sir's care, they were amazed at how many lucky things had actually happened to them.

"It *was* lucky," Violet admitted quietly, "that Klaus invented something so quickly, even though he's not an inventor."

"It *was* lucky," Klaus admitted quietly, "that Violet figured out how to end my hypnosis, even though she's not a researcher."

"Croif," Sunny admitted quietly, which meant something like "It *was* lucky that I could defend us from Dr. Orwell's sword, if I do say so myself."

The children sighed, and gave each other small, hopeful smiles. Count Olaf was on the loose, and would try again to snatch their fortune, but he had not succeeded this time. They were alive, and as they stood together at the broken window, it seemed that the last word on their situation might be "lucky," the word that had caused so much trouble to begin with. The Baudelaire orphans were alive, and it seemed that maybe they had an inordinate amount of luck after all.

LEMONY SNICKET grew up near the sea and currently lives beneath it. To his horror and dismay he has no wife or children, only enemies, associates, and the occasional loyal manservant. His trial has been delayed, so he is free to continue researching and writing the tragic tales of the Baudelaire orphans for Egmont Books.

Email to lemony.snicket@ecb.egmont.com

BRETT HELQUIST was born in Ganado, Arizona, grew up in Orem, Utah, and now lives in New York City. He earned a bachelor's degree in fine arts from Brigham Young University and has been illustrating ever since. His art has appeared in many publications, including *Cricket* magazine and *The New York Times.*

To My Kind Editor,

Please excuse the torn edges of this note. I am
writing to you from inside the shack the
Baudelaire orphans were forced to live in while
at Prufrock Preparatory School, and I am afraid
that some of the crabs tried to snatch my
stationery away from me.

On Sunday night, please purchase a ticket
for seat 10-J at the Erratic Opera Company's
performance of the opera *Faute de Mieux*.
During Act Five, use a sharp knife to rip
open the cushion of your seat. There you
should find my description of the children's
miserable half-semester at boarding school,
entitled THE AUSTERE ACADEMY, as well as a
cafeteria tray, some of the Baudelaires'
handmade staples, and the (worthless) jewel
from Coach Genghis's turban. There is also
the negative for a photograph of the two
Quagmire Triplets, which Mr. Helquist can have
developed to help with his illustrations.

Remember, you are my last hope that the
tales of the Baudelaire orphans can finally be
told to the general public.

With all due respect,

Lemony Snicket

Lemony Snicket